He felt a driving need to protect her.

He tried not to speed on his way back to the cabin, but he didn't like leaving McKenna alone so long. She was making a good show of being stronger, but he'd seen the circles of fatigue under her eyes, the pale tone of her skin. She was still weak, still vulnerable.

About three miles from the turnoff, a glance in the rearview mirror made him sit up straighter. That black SUV about three cars back had been with him since he'd left The Gates, hadn't it?

He took the next turnoff and drove at a steady pace down one of the small feeder roads that led toward Warrior Creek Falls. Only one vehicle behind him followed, keeping a steady distance back. The black SUV.

He was being tailed.

KILLSHADOW ROAD

PAULA GRAVES

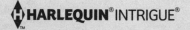

For Jenn, who shares my love for all things Darcy.

Recycling programs
for this product may
not exist in your area.

ISBN-13: 978-0-373-69825-7

Killshadow Road

Copyright © 2015 by Paula Graves

This edition published by arrangement with Harlequin Books S.A.

For questions and comments about the quality of this book,
please contact us at CustomerService@Harlequin.com.

® and TM are trademarks of Harlequin Enterprises Limited or its
corporate affiliates. Trademarks indicated with ® are registered in the
United States Patent and Trademark Office, the Canadian Intellectual
Property Office and in other countries.

Printed in U.S.A.

Paula Graves, an Alabama native, wrote her first book at the age of six. A voracious reader, Paula loves books that pair tantalizing mystery with compelling romance. When she's not reading or writing, she works as a creative director for a Birmingham advertising agency and spends time with her family and friends. Paula invites readers to visit her website, paulagraves.com.

Books by Paula Graves

HARLEQUIN INTRIGUE

The Gates Series

Dead Man's Curve

Crybaby Falls

Boneyard Ridge

Deception Lake

Killshadow Road

Bitterwood PD Series

Murder in the Smokies

The Smoky Mountain Mist

Smoky Ridge Curse

Blood on Copperhead Trail

The Secret of Cherokee Cove

The Legend of Smuggler's Cave

Visit the Author Profile page at Harlequin.com for more titles

CAST OF CHARACTERS

Nick Darcy—The Gates agent is on administrative leave, suspected of having leaked sensitive information that put another operative at risk. But when an old friend shows up on his doorstep injured and hunted, will he put aside his quest to clear his name in order to keep her safe?

McKenna Rigsby—The FBI agent's undercover assignment went very wrong when she learned that someone in the FBI was working with the dangerous militia group she was investigating. Wounded and chased by the bad guys and the good guys alike, she turns to the only person she trusts to watch her back.

Alexander Quinn—The former CIA agent who now runs The Gates gives Darcy his unspoken blessing to protect McKenna. But when the FBI closes in, will he keep her secret?

Cain Dennison—One of Darcy's only friends at The Gates, can he be trusted to help Darcy when his job—and his life—could be on the line?

Cade Landry—The FBI agent working with McKenna on the undercover assignment struck her as apathetic and burned out. Is he the person who set McKenna up?

Ava Solano and Olivia Sharp—The Gates agents who both worked with Landry in the FBI. Will the information they share about Landry make him Darcy's prime suspect?

Darryl Boyle—McKenna's supervisor in the FBI's Knoxville field office has a squeaky-clean background. But does he have secrets nobody's discovered?

Calvin Hopkins—The new head of the Blue Ridge Infantry, a dangerous militia group, is determined to solidify the group's influence among a ruthless criminal organization terrorizing the mountains of eastern Tennessee.

Chapter One

Tablis, Kaziristan, baked beneath the August sunshine, and no amount of joking about it being a dry heat could make the place feel any cooler to the soldiers and diplomats assigned to protect the US Embassy against the rising unrest in the no-man's-land beyond the city walls.

For Nick Darcy, who'd spent most of his childhood in the cool, mild south of England, the brutal summer heat in the Central Asian republic was a shock to the system. The dress code for his job with the Diplomatic Security Service—suit, tie, holstered weapon—didn't help.

But the escalating tensions in the Kaziristan countryside had driven considerations such as climate and comfort from the minds of everyone tasked with the embassy's protection.

Something was building. Something bad. Darcy could feel it as if it were a living creature writhing beneath the dusty earth, making the very ground beneath his feet feel unsteady.

Trouble was coming. Fast and hard.

A harsh squawk of static from his handheld radio jangled his nerves. "BOGART on the move."

Darcy acknowledged the signal and watched from his post for the ambassador's car to emerge through the slowly opening gates. The dusty black sedan moved safely through the opening and onto the four-lane boulevard in front of the embassy. The sedan made it down the road about thirty yards before all hell broke loose.

A rocket-propelled grenade slammed into the ambassador's car and sent pieces flying through the air. One slab of metal debris slammed into the stone column next to Darcy, fragmenting the stone and sending a large chunk slamming into his forehead.

Staggered by the blow, he held on to the column to stay upright and tried to see through the blood pouring into his eyes. The road in front of the embassy was suddenly teeming with armed men and even more young men throwing rocks and swinging clubs.

The embassy was under siege.

Darcy managed to get his pistol out of his holster, but his movements felt slow and awkward, as if he couldn't quite convince his limbs to do what he asked of them.

A pair of small but strong hands wrapped around his arm and pulled. "Move it, Darcy! We're under siege!"

He turned to look at the speaker, tried to focus on her small, freckled face and her sharp green eyes, but the world seemed to be spinning out of control, around and around until black spots started to appear in his vision.

She muttered a profanity and started yelling for help in that hillbilly accent of hers that always made him smile. He tried to smile now, but his face felt paralyzed.

Nothing made sense. Not anymore.

His world fragmented into a thousand shards of light, then faded into nothing.

Nick Darcy woke to the sort of darkness that one found miles from a big city. No ambient light tempered the deep gloom, and the only noise was the sound of his heart pounding a rapid cadence of panic against his breastbone.

Only a dream.

Except it hadn't been. The embassy siege had happened. People had died, some in the most brutal ways imaginable.

And he'd been unable to save them.

He pushed the stem of his watch, lighting up the dial. Four in the morning. As he sat up and reached for the switch of the lamp on the table beside him, he heard a soft thump outside the cabin. His nerves, still in fight-or-flight mode, vibrated like the taut strings of a violin.

Leaving the light off, he reached for his SIG Sauer P229 and eased it from the holster lying on the coffee table in front of the sofa.

The noises could be coming from a scavenging raccoon venturing onto the cabin porch or the wind knocking a dead limb from one of the blight-ridden Fraser firs surrounding his cabin.

But between his years with the DSS and the past year he'd been working for Alexander Quinn at The Gates, he knew that bumps in the night could also mean deadly trouble.

As he moved silently toward the front door, he heard another sound from outside. A soft thump against the door, half knock, half scrape.

There was no security lens set into the heavy wood front door of the cabin, a failing he made a mental note to rectify as soon as possible. He improvised, edging toward the window that looked out onto the porch and angling his gaze toward the welcome mat in front of the door.

The view was obstructed by the angle, but he thought he could make out a dark mass lying on the porch.

He checked the SIG's magazine and chambered a round before he pulled open the front door.

A woman spilled inside and crumpled at his feet.

Fearing a trick, Darcy swept the porch with his gaze and his SIG until reassured the woman at his feet was his only visitor. Crouching next to her, he didn't touch her at first, looking for any signs of a booby trap or some sort of body-worn explosive.

Instead, he found blood. A lot of it, seeping through the woman's dark sweater and leaving a smear on the hardwood floor of the cabin.

In the dark, he couldn't make out much more about her except that she was small and slimly built, with a mass of curly hair that seemed to wrap itself around his fingers like a living creature as he pushed it aside to take a look at the face hidden beneath.

Even in the gloom, there was no mistaking the belligerent round chin or small, slightly snub nose.

"Rigsby?"

She stirred at the sound of his voice, her eyes opening enough for him to catch the slight glitter of reflected moonlight before her eyelids fluttered closed.

He pushed to his feet and flicked the light switch by the door, squinting against the sudden brightness. Illumination only made things seem more dire, he observed as he knelt beside McKenna Rigsby's still body and checked her vitals.

Her pulse was stronger and steadier than he'd anticipated. Good sign. The blood on her sweater, while sufficient in quantity to be alarming, seemed limited to only that one spot near her rib cage. He eased the sweater up and away from her skin, revealing a pair of bullet holes in the soft tissue of her left side, beneath the rib cage but above the curve of her hip. Not a large caliber, he saw with relief. The bullet had gone in and out without leaving a large exit wound.

Still, she needed medical attention, and soon.

Well, as soon as EMTs from town could get out to this stretch of wilderness in the Smoky Mountain foothills.

What was McKenna doing here? Had she come here looking for him after all these years?

Questions can wait. Find the phone. Call 911.

As he started to rise, McKenna's hand snaked out and

grabbed his, keeping him crouched beside her. Her eyelids opened to reveal bright green eyes dark with pain. "Don't trust anyone."

"What?"

"Don't trust anyone. Don't call a doctor." Her grasp weakened, her hand slipping away to fall with a soft thud to the floor. Her eyelids shut again, and she was out once more.

At any other point in his life, he'd have ignored her whispered commands and called 911 anyway. But the past few years had taught him a hell of a lot more than he wanted to know about treachery. He was on suspension from The Gates because of someone's treachery, with no access and no way to find out who was trying to destroy his life.

Tugging the sweater up again, he looked more closely at the bullet wounds, trying to remember everything he knew about field triage. Her pulse was still strong and steady, and the blood on her sweater, while a gory mess, wasn't more than a couple of pints. As long as no vital organs or blood vessels had been hit, she could survive that much loss of blood if he could stop the bleeding and rehydrate her.

The bullet holes in her side were only a half inch or so from the curve of her abdomen, so it was possible the bullet had gone through flesh only, missing any organs.

But why was she unconscious?

He checked her head, ignoring the way her curls tangled around his fingers as he gently probed her skull for any sign of a head injury. He felt no bumps, no cuts or abrasions, nothing to suggest she'd taken any sort of blow to the head. He sat back on his heels and observed her for a second.

She appeared thin. Thinner than he remembered, certainly. Her skin was naturally fair, but the darkened shadows beneath her eyes gave him an uneasy feeling in the pit of his stomach.

"Rigsby?"

Her eyelids fluttered open. "Hi."

He smiled. "Hi. Can you stick around this time and tell me what happened?"

"I'm tired." Her eyes started to close again.

He gave her a light shake, earning a grimace of displeasure from his patient. "If I'm going to do what you asked and not call a doctor, I need you to give me a good reason for my restraint."

Her eyes snapped open again, meeting his steadily for the first time. "Darcy."

"Rigsby."

Her lips curved slightly at his dry response. "Of all the cabins in all the Podunk little mountain towns…"

"You had to fall headfirst into mine."

"I knew you lived here." She made the admission as if she was a little embarrassed. "I didn't know who else to trust. Not even sure I can trust you, but I need help, so…"

"How bad are the gunshot wounds? Can you tell?"

"I don't think it hit anything major." She tried to rise, grimacing with the effort.

He helped her into a sitting position. "Define *major*."

She looked up at him through a tangle of auburn curls that had fallen over her forehead. "No internal organs or major blood vessels compromised."

"Are you certain?"

"I've been running through the woods for six hours and I haven't bled out yet."

Six hours? She'd been in this condition for six hours? "Do you know who shot you?"

She shook her head no. "Not a clue. Which is why I can't trust anyone." She pushed her hair back with one shaky hand, meeting his gaze. "I'm hoping I can trust you."

"You can," he said firmly. "We need to stop the bleeding."

She looked down at her side, her lips curling in dismay. "That's gonna leave a scar."

"Never knew you to be vain, Rigsby."

She looked at him from beneath a furrowed brow. "Been so long out of the DSS that you've forgotten what battle-field humor sounds like?"

He didn't feel like smiling. "Why would someone be shooting you, McKenna?"

She made a face at his use of her first name. "I was looking into something. For thc FBI. I guess I got too close."

"Too close to what?"

She looked down at her bloody hands. "Do you think we could get me cleaned up a little before I undergo the post-mission debriefing, Agent Darcy?"

"I'm not with the DSS anymore."

She slanted him a look of pure irritation. "Yes, I know."

"Keeping up with my career, Rigsby?" He helped her to her feet, keeping his hands on her arms until he was sure she wouldn't topple over if he let go. "I'm touched."

She pulled her arms free of his grasp and took a stagger-ing step back before she regained her balance. "Purgatory is in my new jurisdiction," she said coolly. "I was assigned to the Knoxville Field Office a few months ago."

"After the incident at the Tri-State Law Enforcement Society conference?"

"As a matter of fact, yes." She tugged the edge of her bloody sweater down to cover her wounds, wincing. "I really need to sit down."

Muttering a soft curse, he crossed to where she stood and picked her up, tightening his grip against her weak strug-gles. "Stop fighting me and I'll let you go soon enough."

He carried her through the narrow hallway into the cabin's main bathroom and set her on the counter of the long double-sink cabinet. She looked around the spacious room, one ginger-brown eyebrow cocking upward. "Nice digs."

"It came with the job." Most of the men and women who

worked for Alexander Quinn had no idea that he owned about half the real estate in the foothills just east of Purgatory, including almost fifty rental cabins that brought in a generous income beyond his profits from The Gates. While the security and investigation agency was doing remarkably brisk business for a new company, the kind of high-tech services The Gates offered weren't inexpensive. But Quinn was a wealthy man in his own right, and if he had chosen to funnel his own money into the company, who was Darcy to question his wisdom?

"Looks like one of those tourist-honeymoon cabins." She nodded at the ridiculously large claw-foot tub. "Is your bed heart-shaped?"

"You'll see for yourself once you've cleaned up and re-hydrated."

"I could kill for a strong cup of coffee." She winced again as he tugged the hem of her sweater up to take another look at her wounds.

"We'll start with water and see how that goes." He opened the drawer of the sink cabinet and pulled out a clean washcloth. "First, we need to clean your wounds and get them disinfected."

"Don't suppose you know a crooked pharmacist we could bribe for some antibiotics?" she asked as he turned on the hot-water tap and let the water soak the washcloth.

"Sadly, no, though I could probably throw a stick in any direction and hit a methamphetamine dealer."

"We call 'em 'meth mechanics' or 'meth cookers' around here," she said, a smile in her voice despite the obvious pain creasing her forehead. "I will say you've lost a little of your accent since the last time I saw you."

"Perish the thought." He wrung some of the excess water from the washcloth before adding a dollop of antibiotic hand soap to the rag. "Not quite Betadine, but—"

"Ow!" She sucked in a harsh breath, making him feel like a brute.

"Sorry," he murmured, trying to take it easier on her.

"No, don't be gentle. The cleaner you get it, the less likely I'll end up in a hospital on an IV." She twisted to give him better access to her injury, moaning a little as he washed the ragged edges of the bullet wounds.

"You're likely to end up hospitalized no matter what I do," he warned as he rinsed blood from the used washcloth and dug into the drawer for a fresh one. "Why is it that you think there's no one you can trust?"

Instead of answering his question, she leaned forward, resting her forehead on his shoulder. Her low alto drawl came out weak and strained. "Hold off a second, okay?"

He put his hand on the back of her head, his fingers tangling in her curls. Her skin was hot and damp, and her breath burned against his throat when she turned her head toward him.

"I was so afraid you wouldn't be here," she murmured.

"I'm here." He stroked her hair, fighting against an old familiar ache of longing. McKenna Rigsby had twisted him into knots once, a long time ago, and it had taken years to untangle himself.

"I know you have every reason to be mad at me, Darcy," she whispered against his collarbone. "I wouldn't blame you if you tossed me back into the woods to fend for myself."

"I would never do that."

She lifted her head, gazing up at him with pain-dark eyes. She lifted one bloodstained hand to his face. "I know. That's why I came to you."

He couldn't stop himself from bending to touch his forehead to hers. Her breath came out in an explosive little whoosh, mingling with his ragged respiration. "You'll be the death of me yet, Rigsby."

"I never wanted to hurt you, Darcy. That's why—" Her

words ended on a soft sigh. "I don't like to need people. You know that."

All too well. "But you need me now."

She pulled back, her gaze intense. "I do. I need your help."

"You have it."

To his surprise, tears welled in her eyes. She brushed them away with her knuckles. "Ready to give this torture another go?"

He reached for the hot washcloth and the hand soap. "Are you?"

She stripped her sweater over her head, tossing the bloody garment onto the floor, revealing her bra and a holster on her right hip the sweater had hidden. She tugged the holster free and laid it on the counter, the Glock 27 gleaming.

Bending to expose her side to him, she told him, "Finish it."

He cleaned the wounds a second time, making sure to remove anything that looked like debris from the raw skin. The bleeding had nearly stopped, he saw with relief. If he could get a few pints of water into her, she should recover from the blood loss soon enough.

He washed the blood from his own hands and opened the cabinet over the nearest sink. He had a prepackaged first-aid kit stored there, though he wasn't sure the maker had planned for a medical emergency that included bullet wounds. There were better kits stocked at The Gates, but he was on paid leave from the agency at the moment. He could hardly sneak in and spirit out supplies without someone taking notice.

Pulling out the best tools available—antiseptic wipes, antibiotic ointment, sterile gauze pads and some surgical tape—he treated and bandaged the wounds as quickly and efficiently as he could. "The sweater is a loss, I fear."

"Just lend me a T-shirt." She slanted an amused look at him as she picked up her weapon and holster. "You do own one, don't you?"

"Several, actually." He helped her down from the sink counter, trying to ignore the silky heat of her bare skin beneath his fingers. She wobbled a little, and he slipped his arm around her shoulders, keeping her upright as they left the bathroom and headed down the narrow hall to his bedroom.

As he dug in the large chest of drawers in the corner for a clean shirt for her, she eyed his large bed with a hint of dismay. "Not heart-shaped."

"Sadly, no." He handed her a black T-shirt and a long-sleeved fleece jacket. "It'll get cold in the night."

"Where are you going to sleep?" She eased the T-shirt over her head with a grimace.

"The sofa in my study is comfortable."

"I should take it." She swayed a little, her face paler than usual.

He caught her before she collapsed, easing her down to the bed. "Let's get you under the covers." He pulled back the blanket and helped her slide between the sheets. Tucking the blanket up around her, he added, "We need to get some fluids back into you. Think you could handle soup or some broth as well as water?"

She caught his hand as he started to rise. "Wait. First, I need to tell you something." Her voice faltered, and her eyes began to droop again. "There's a reason you can't trust anyone. You can't let anyone know I'm here. Not even someone you trust."

"What the hell is going on, Rigsby?" He cradled her

face between his palms, not liking the flushed heat rising in her cheeks. "Who is after you?"

"I'm not sure exactly," she admitted, her eyes fluttering to stay open. "But I know it's someone I work with."

He frowned. "Someone you work with?"

Her gaze steadied, locking with his. "Whoever shot me was working with someone in the FBI."

Chapter Two

McKenna could see the wheels in Nick Darcy's mind turning at turbo speed. Despite his recent clashes with hidebound bureaucracy, she knew there would always be a part of Darcy that tried to play by the rules. He'd grown up in a Foreign Service household, where protocol and diplomacy reigned, and not even the past few months of work as a private security contractor had freed him from those constraints.

"Someone in the FBI?" He dropped his hands away from her face and rose from the bed.

"You say that as if you'd never seen government corruption." Her whole left side was beginning to ache like a bad tooth, and her throat felt dry and scratchy. "I don't suppose we could discuss this further over a gallon of water and some ibuprofen?"

"Of course." He disappeared through the bedroom door as if a horde of rogue FBI agents were after him.

She fell back against the pillows of his bed and stared up at the exposed beams of the ceiling, trying to pretend she didn't feel like one big bloody wound. She was in a safe place, for now at least, which was a hell of a lot better position than she'd been in just an hour ago.

Only a handful in the FBI knew the dangerous game she'd been playing for the past three months. One of them had put her in the crosshairs of a deadly group of domestic terrorists and given them the go-ahead to pull the trigger. Literally.

But who?

Darcy returned to the bedroom carrying a wicker basket. When he set it on the bed and opened the latch at the top, McKenna saw it was exactly what it looked like—a picnic basket containing a large bottle of water, a metal thermos and a bottle of ibuprofen tablets.

"I didn't think you'd want anything heavy, so the soup is just chicken broth. I packed a few crackers in there if you want them." He set the water bottle on the bedside table next to her. "How long since you last ate?"

She rubbed her gritty eyes. "Yesterday. I had a protein bar around dinnertime, I think."

He went still, his hand closed around the top of the vacuum flask. His dark eyes slanted to meet hers. "How long have you been running, Rigsby?"

"Two days."

Slowly, he withdrew the thermos and sleeve of crackers from the basket and set them on the night table beside the water. He picked up the bottle of pain-reliever tablets and set the basket on the floor before he sat down beside her.

"You've been running for two days."

She tried to push up to a sitting position, biting her lip at the hard arc of pain that rushed down her side in response.

Darcy leaned forward and wrapped his arms around her, pulling her upright until they sat in an approximation of an intimate embrace.

Except, it didn't feel like an approximation. It felt right. So right.

Darcy's arms fell away too soon, and he sat back, his eyes fathomless. "What sent you on the run?"

"It's a really long story."

His eyes narrowed slightly. "One you don't intend to share with me?"

"I didn't say that."

"Here." He leaned forward, his chest brushing against her shoulder as he picked up the thermos. As he removed the top, the fragrant steam of hot broth drifted past her nose, igniting a storm of hunger in the pit of her empty stomach. "Eat. Then sleep. We can talk when you're stronger."

Watching him pour broth into the cap of the thermos, she sighed. "I will tell you everything I know, Darcy."

His gaze angled to meet hers. "Yes. You will."

The firmness of his tone should have irritated her. Instead, it sent a flutter of relief rolling through her, as if she'd finally reached the solid shore after an endless battle with a raging sea.

He gave her the thermos lid that doubled as a mug. "Drink."

She drank a few swallows of the hot broth, trying not to shiver as warmth spread through her insides and started to warm her chilled bones. Darcy picked up the bottle of ibuprofen, shook out a couple of tablets and handed them to her. "Want the water or can you swallow them down with the broth?"

She took the tablets and washed them down with a couple of gulps of broth. "Thank you."

"You are safe here, Rigsby. You know that, don't you?" There was a soft tone to Darcy's voice that she'd rarely heard in all the time she'd known him. She looked up to find him watching her from beneath a furrowed brow.

"As safe as I am anywhere," she agreed.

His hand moved toward her, just a few inches, before falling back in his lap. She felt an answering tug low in her belly, a sensation so familiar it made her want to cry.

How long had she been fighting against the pull of him? As long as she'd known him?

The siege in Kaziristan had happened almost eight years ago. She'd been a rookie FBI agent, fresh out of law school and the Academy. Her first overseas assignment had landed her in the middle of a brewing civil uprising, working as an assistant in the FBI Legal Attaché Office in Tablis—the legat, in bureau parlance. The legat's primary missions in Tablis had been to train the local police forces in counterterrorism strategies and to aid in the investigation of crimes against US citizens, especially embassy personnel.

She'd gotten a quick and brutal lesson in both during her time in Kaziristan. So had Nick Darcy.

"Do you still see people from Tablis?" she asked as she reached for the sleeve of crackers he'd set on the nightstand.

He got there first, pulling open the airtight packaging and holding it out for her to retrieve a couple of crackers. "Sometimes. I ran into Maddox Heller a few years ago in the Caribbean."

"Wow, that's a blast from the past." She nibbled the edge of one of the crackers. "Y'all so shafted him after the siege."

Darcy's expression tightened. "I had nothing to do with it."

"Right. It was all Barton Reid, I guess?" She grimaced. Marine Security Guard Maddox Heller had saved dozens of lives during the siege in Tablis, but the State Department had made him a scapegoat for the security mistakes made at the embassy.

"It wasn't all Reid's doing. But he was the instigator, yes."

"I knew he was a snake. Didn't shed a tear when I heard he got life for his crimes." She sipped some more broth. "How was Heller when you saw him?"

"He was living life as a beach bum."

She winced. "That bad?"

"*Beach bum* is perhaps an exaggeration." Darcy's lips curved, almost forming a smile. "He'd inherited a good deal of money and invested well. But he dressed atrociously, worked questionable jobs and frequented shady establishments, so—"

"The horror."

His lips tilted farther upward. "He's married now. Moved back to the States to be with the woman. Has a young daughter." There was more to Maddox Heller's story he wasn't sharing, she saw, but she didn't push. Another lesson she'd learned from her year in Kaziristan—some secrets needed to remain unspoken. Lives could depend on it.

"Good for him." She made herself swallow the remaining broth in the thermos cup before she set it on the nightstand next to the flask. "How's Quinn?"

"Largely unchanged." A hint of irritation edged his voice.

"He's the one who put you on administrative leave?"

His gaze snapped to meet hers. "How do you know about that?"

"We're the FBI. We hear things."

The annoyed expression that came over his face was so familiar she could barely suppress a smile. "There's an internal investigation into an information leak."

"Right. A leak about what?"

He arched an eyebrow. "I'm not the leak."

She reached across the space between them and put her hand on his arm. His gaze darkened, but he didn't look away. "I know you're not."

He pressed his hand over hers briefly, then moved her hand away and stood. "I'll leave everything here in case you get thirsty later. Call out if you need me. I'll be listening."

"Thank you." A sense of calm reassurance swamped her suddenly, making tears of relief prick her eyes. She hadn't been sure, even to the last second before Darcy opened the door, that she'd made the right decision coming here. But now she knew her instincts had been correct.

Nick Darcy might not like her very much these days. He probably didn't trust her, at least on a personal basis, at all.

But he was still the only person she trusted to have her back in a crisis.

HE WAS HARBORING a woman with bullet wounds in her side. An FBI agent, to be exact, a woman who now claimed that someone in her own agency had targeted her for murder and nearly succeeded.

"Bloody hell," he murmured, dropping onto the sofa in his study and sinking into the comfortable cushions, his mind racing a mile a minute.

His first instinct, he realized with some surprise, was to call Alexander Quinn. Only a few years back, his instinct would have been quite the opposite.

The trill of his cell phone sent a jangle of nerves jarring their way up his spine. He grabbed the phone from the nearby desk and shook his head as he saw the name on the display. "What is it, Quinn?"

"I've received notice of an APB out for an FBI agent suspected of aiding and abetting a domestic terrorist group."

Darcy went still. "And you're telling me this because?"

"We know her. From Kaziristan."

There had been only one female FBI agent in the legat in Tablis. "McKenna Rigsby?"

"That's the one."

"Aiding and abetting a domestic terrorist group how?"

"The information I received didn't say, and I didn't ask." Quinn's voice deepened. "She attended that law enforcement conference the Blue Ridge Infantry infiltrated a few months ago. Maybe they had more people on the inside than we realized at the time."

"And you're telling me all of this now because?"

"Because the last time anyone saw her, she was crossing Killshadow Road, about a mile from your place."

Darcy tightened his grip on the phone, his skin prickling with alarm. She was spotted so near? It must have been a recent sighting. Searchers were probably close by.

Would they want to search his place?

"I haven't seen her since Kaziristan," he lied. "And I doubt she'd care to see me again, considering how strained our acquaintance had become by the time we parted ways."

"You never told me what happened."

"No, I didn't."

"You will contact me if you spot her?" Quinn asked.

"You're first on my speed dial."

If Quinn noticed his reply was hardly an affirmative answer, he didn't respond. In fact, he said nothing else before he disconnected the call.

Darcy released a pent-up breath and set the phone on the desk as he rose and crossed to the window. Killshadow Road was the only regular road leading into this part of the woods. Gravel and dirt roads branched off the paved road for a stretch of five or six miles, some leading to occupied cabins, while others ended in grown-over plots of land where cabins had once stood.

Back during the boom period for the area, when the Smoky Mountains became a tourist destination for people in the southeastern United States, entrepreneurs had tried to capitalize on the desire for short-term mountain living, and tourist cabins and resorts had begun to dot the landscape for miles just outside the national park's perimeter. Some of those resorts had thrived, especially those easily accessed from the interstate and major highways.

Others, like Purgatory, Tennessee, had never caught the imagination of the tourists.

It was a shame, Darcy thought, because there was a lot to recommend the little town in the middle of nowhere.

"Was that Quinn on the phone?"

The sound of McKenna's faint voice sent a little thrill

of awareness rushing up his spine to spread like tingles through his brain. He turned and saw, with dismay, that she was as pale as a winter sky and barely upright, leaning against the door frame.

He crossed quickly to her side and wrapped his arm around her waist, taking care to avoid the site of her wounds. "What are you doing out of bed?"

"He told you, didn't he?" Her breath warmed his neck and stirred the hair behind his ear, sending a different sort of tingle coursing through him. He ignored the bad timing of his libido and helped her back to the bedroom.

"If you mean he told me you're wanted by the FBI, then yes. He did."

She slumped back against the pillows, looking defeated. "You told him I'm here. Didn't you." It wasn't a question.

He tucked the covers up around her. "I didn't. I should have, God knows. But I don't think he wanted to know."

Her brow furrowed. "What do you mean?"

"If Quinn wanted to know if you were here, he'd have stopped by to see for himself. Instead, he wanted to get me some information I needed, in case you *were* here."

"That's ridiculously convoluted," she muttered.

"That's Quinn." He smoothed the blanket beside her. "He believes you're being railroaded. And he wants me to do anything possible to protect you."

She levered herself upward to a half-sitting position, grimacing. "What do *you* believe?"

"I believe you're in trouble."

Her eyes narrowed, and he saw his halfhearted answer had struck a blow. She looked away and finished sitting up. "I can go." She plucked at the hem of the borrowed shirt. "Can I keep the tee? My sweater is a loss."

He closed his hands over her arms, holding her in place when she started to edge toward the other side of the bed. "Don't be stupid."

"Don't be insulting." She shook off his hands.

"I don't think you've hooked up with a domestic terror group."

"Wow, thanks for that vote of confidence."

"But I know how little you care for the rules if you think they'll stop you from getting the outcome you want." He kept his tone gentle, though there was an edge of bitterness he couldn't quite keep out of his voice.

"And I know how piously you worship them," she shot back.

"We had to follow the evacuation protocols."

"And Cameron died!" Her voice rose to a point before dropping to a hoarse half whisper. "He died because we left him behind."

He pushed down a surge of guilt and kept his voice as even as he dared. "I know that. I never, ever forget that."

"We could've—" Her voice broke, and he knew she was thinking the same thing he was. If they'd stayed to save Cameron from the fire, they'd have died, too. That part of the embassy had collapsed seconds after they cleared the area. Lingering one minute more would have been certain death for all three of them.

"No, we couldn't. And I know you'll never forgive me for pulling you out of there. I can live with that." He put one finger under her chin and tipped her face up, willing her to look at him.

Her eyes drifted closed, refusing to comply.

He dropped his hand away. "I know that whatever you've done, whatever you're doing now, is something you believe is right. Whatever rules you've broken, whatever orders you've defied, you've done it with good intentions. That's what I believe."

Slowly, she opened her eyes and looked at him, fire in her expression. She spoke slowly and carefully, her accent disappearing with her precise pronunciation. "I broke the rules, Darcy, because someone in the FBI was aware I was getting close to discovering their link to the Blue Ridge Infantry and their hodgepodge of associates. Those people have gone beyond meth dealing and planting pipe bombs. They are up to something huge. Mass-casualty huge. And someone in the FBI is facilitating their plans."

"And you don't know who?"

"Six people in the FBI knew I was trying to infiltrate the Blue Ridge Infantry. One of them set me up. I just don't know which one."

She looked even paler than before, he realized, except for the bruise-like purple shadows beneath her haunted eyes. He hated what he was about to say but he had no choice. Quinn's call had been a clear signal.

"I know you're tired. Clearly you need rest."

"I'm okay—"

"No, you're not." He reached over to the nightstand and picked up the thermos. He checked to make sure the seal was tight before he put it in the wicker basket on the floor at his feet. "But this can't be helped."

"What are you doing?"

"Packing," he said as he reached for the water bottle and checked the top, as well. "We have to leave this cabin now. Before the people out there looking for you realize you came here."

Chapter Three

"How are you holding up?"

Darcy's low voice rumbled like thunder through her pain-hazed mind, stirring her from a jumble of disjointed dreams. All she could remember of those fractured images was the loamy smell of decaying leaves on the forest floor beneath her nose as she hid from a horde of faceless shadows chasing her through the woods.

She twisted her head to look at him. "How do you think?"

"You look like bloody hell."

"You're so free with the compliments, Darcy. People will talk." She realized they weren't moving. Looking up, she saw they were in a line of cars waiting for a stoplight to change colors. "Where are we?"

"Just south of Bitterwood."

"Where's that?"

"Just south of Purgatory."

"And where's that?"

"Somewhere north of hell." Darcy's lips quirked at the corners. "I think you'd be safe to take some acetaminophen now if you think it'll help with the pain. Your ibuprofen dose was nearly two hours ago."

She shook her head. "No more pain relievers. They're making me feel loopy and that's worse than the pain."

He pressed the back of his hand to her cheek, catching her off guard. She slanted a questioning look toward him and he dropped his hand away. "Over-the-counter pain relievers shouldn't be making you feel loopy. You're a little warm for my liking."

She shifted in her seat, sucking in a quick gasp at the ache in her injured side. "You think I have a fever?"

"Maybe. I don't have time to get the first-aid kit out." Ahead, the light had turned green and they started moving again. "We'll be there soon and I'll take your temperature and see where we are."

"Where is 'there'?" She fought to keep her eyes open, weary of the nightmares that chased her through her dreams when she drifted off.

"It's a cabin. Belongs to someone I work with."

"Quinn?"

"No. Someone else. He's out of town for a week. Took his sister and his fiancée to the beach to celebrate. His cabin is empty for the next few days, and it's deep in the woods, far enough from here that no one should bother us."

Even through the haze of pain, mention of a trip to the beach caught her attention. "Are you talking about Hunter Bragg?"

He angled a sharp look toward her. "You know Bragg?"

"I know his fiancée. She's my cousin. I talked to her a couple of weeks ago, before everything in my undercover op started going belly-up." She quirked one corner of her mouth. "Pear-shaped, I think you Brits call it."

"Not a Brit," he murmured, but his lips curved upward. It was an old joke between them, one she hadn't been certain he'd remember after all this time.

He was technically as American as she was. He just sounded like his British-born mother after spending his formative years in England.

"Did you tell Hunter what's going on?" she asked after his smile faded.

"Of course not."

"So we're breaking in and staking out squatters' rights for a few days while he's away?"

"Yes."

"That sounds a whole lot like breaking the rules, Darcy."

"I like to live life on the edge." His dry tone made her laugh, which she instantly regretted.

"Ow," she moaned, shifting to find a more comfortable position.

"We're close," he promised her, and sure enough, within a few minutes he had turned the Land Rover off the main highway onto a one-lane road that twisted and turned deep into the woods.

The one lane ended abruptly in the middle of nowhere, and for a second, McKenna thought they'd taken a wrong turn. But at the last second, Darcy steered the Land Rover onto a narrow dirt road the woods seemed to swallow whole.

The road twisted and climbed until they appeared to be a long way from anything approaching civilization. Then the dirt road disappeared, and Darcy stopped the Land Rover and turned off the engine.

McKenna gazed into the dense thicket of trees in front of them, her heart sinking. "Where's the cabin?"

"Through those trees."

She felt sick at the thought of trudging through the woods again so soon. "Don't suppose we could just stay here? Bunk down in the back?"

"I promise, it's not far." He unbuckled his seat belt and got out of the SUV, walked around the front and opened the passenger door. His dark eyes met hers steadily. "You can do this."

Gritting her teeth, she unbuckled her own seat belt and eased her legs toward the open door, trying to ignore the burning ache in her side. "If anyone ever says 'It's just a flesh wound' to me again, I swear I'm going to belt them right in the mouth."

He held out his hands. She took them and let him help her to the ground. Her legs felt like noodles, but she willed herself to stay upright, not wanting to show any weakness in front of Darcy. If she couldn't convince him she was on the mend, he would ignore her wishes and follow his own instincts to call in help.

And if he did that, they both might end up dead.

McKenna had gone from pasty white to a sickly gray color by the time the evergreen trees gave way with shocking suddenness to a narrow clearing that housed a small, rustic-looking cabin. Darcy slid his arm around her shoulders and felt her tremble under his touch.

"Thank God," she murmured, leaning her head briefly against his shoulder before she started to move again.

"It's hardly the Waldorf," he warned as he helped her up the three steps to the cabin porch and settled her in one of the two cane-bottom rockers that sat to the right of the door.

"Whatever."

He wasn't sure she'd be so blasé about the cabin's primitive comforts. The owner, Hunter Bragg, didn't live there full-time, but it was apparently a favorite getaway for him and his new fiancée, if office scuttlebutt was anything to go by.

There was no easily discovered spare key to be had, Darcy was certain. The Gates trained their agents not to be careless.

But the agency also taught their agents to be skilled and

resourceful. Darcy pulled a lock-pick kit from his backpack and made quick work of the dead bolt on the front door.

"That is so illegal," McKenna murmured, sounding impressed.

He shot her a quick smile. "I am not the man you knew in Kaziristan."

"I'm beginning to see that." She pushed herself up from the rocker, wobbling a little when she gained her feet.

He caught her elbow in his firm grasp and led her into the dark cabin.

The power was running, though all the lights and appliances had been turned off, leaving the cabin's interior shadowed in the early-morning gloom. Darcy flicked the light switch on, and the overhead lamps revealed a small, cold front room furnished with an old but sturdy-looking sofa, what looked like an old Army footlocker doubling as a coffee table, and a couple of mismatched armchairs that sat across from the sofa to create a shabby but cozy conversation area.

"Are you cold?" he asked, nodding toward the fireplace.

She followed his gaze, one eyebrow arching as she saw that, instead of logs, the width of the hearth was filled with a large electric space heater. "Well. *That's* different."

"Apparently the point of this backwoods haven is maximum seclusion and secrecy. I suppose smoke rising from the chimney would negate that effect." He took her arm and eased her over to the sofa. "Sit. I'll retrieve the rest of the supplies from the Land Rover."

By the time he returned with the two large duffel bags he and McKenna had stuffed full of supplies they might need, McKenna had curled up into a miserable-looking knot on the sofa.

"You look ill," he commented as he set the duffels on the floor.

"You're such a sweet talker, Darcy. I bet all the ladies love you."

He ignored her soft gibe and crossed to her side, placing the back of his hand against her cheek. She was definitely warmer than she'd been in the car. And she'd been quite warm then.

"I need to take a look at your wounds."

She managed a grimace of a smile. "Is that a proposition?"

"It's a statement of fact. You appear to be feverish. If your wounds are infected, we need to alter our plan."

"We had a plan?" she asked through gritted teeth as she plucked the hem of his T-shirt away from her side.

Blood had oozed through the gauze bandage, he saw, though not a lot. He eased the bandage away from her torn skin and took in the two holes in her flesh. The skin around them was reddened and warm to the touch. "I'm afraid infection may be setting in."

"Clean it again," she said. "Just give me a bullet to bite first."

"You need antibiotics. We need to get you to a physician."

"Can't do that," she said with a firm shake of her head. "Any other ideas?"

One, but he didn't particularly like it. "I could break into the free clinic in Bitterwood and steal some antibiotics."

She stared at him in stunned silence for a moment. "You are definitely not the man I knew in Kaziristan."

He wasn't. He hadn't been for a long time.

"Is there an option between those two extremes?" she asked when he said nothing else.

He nodded. "I can call on someone I trust for help."

"He hasn't made contact again, has he?"

Alexander Quinn looked up from his laptop computer

and found Olivia Sharp standing in the doorway of his office, her shoulder leaning against the door frame. Her bare, shapely legs seemed to rise for miles before disappearing beneath the charcoal pencil skirt of her lightweight summer suit. She was a tall woman who didn't need to wear heels to be imposing, but today's footwear sported four-inch heels and open toes that displayed the impertinent bright green of her toenail polish.

"He has not," he answered her question. "Have you anything new to report?"

She shook her head as she entered the office and closed the door. "Anson Daughtry has taken advantage of his administrative leave to drive down to Atlanta for something called The Mixed Magic Tour. Five alt-punk bands on one stage, lots of alcohol and girls with rainbow-colored hair." She shrugged. "Are you sure he's thirty-two?"

Quinn tamped down a smile. "Almost thirty-three."

"Either he's not concerned about the internal investigation or he's trying very hard to appear unconcerned." Olivia shot Quinn a shrewd look. "I'm leaning toward the latter."

Quinn concurred. "What about the agent you assigned to him?"

"He can hardly follow him to Atlanta. Daughtry would spot him." Olivia sat in the chair across from Quinn's desk and crossed one long leg over the other. "I take it Darcy hasn't sent out a distress signal to the other agent?"

"Not yet."

"How did he sound when you talked to him earlier?"

"Worried. And wary."

She nodded. "To be expected."

"You haven't told me which man you most suspect of being the mole."

"I consider everyone a suspect at the moment." She arched one honey-brown eyebrow. "Even you."

He smiled at that. "Anything new on the FBI angle?"

"I'm not exactly the bureau's favorite former denizen."

"Still, you worked for the FBI for almost eight years. Surely there's a contact left you can exploit."

Her brow furrowed, and he realized he'd touched a nerve. "I've put out some feelers."

He frowned at her wary tone. "What aren't you telling me?"

"I've told you everything I know pertinent to this case."

"The next time you bother to come to my office to talk, I expect you to be the one supplying information. Clear?"

Her full lips thinned with annoyance. "Yes, sir." She rose like a waterbird taking flight, all long legs and soaring, restless spirit. She stalked to the door in three long strides, then turned at the last moment to look at him.

"I'm going to find out who's leaking information from this agency, Quinn. No matter who it is. How's that for a little useful information?" Before he could respond, she was out the door, letting it shut with a loud snap behind her.

Quinn sat back in his chair, regarded the closed door and unsuccessfully tried to stifle a smile.

His intercom buzzed. Line four—Dennison. He felt a flutter of anticipation as he picked up the phone. "Tell me you've got something."

Cain Dennison's gravelly voice held a hint of irritation. Quinn knew the agent didn't care for spying on one of his own, even in an attempt to clear his name. "He called two minutes ago."

"What did he want?"

"He wants a few minutes alone with my grandmother."

"She's a what?" McKenna stared at Darcy, certain she'd misunderstood.

"A sort of mountain healer, if the stories are true." Darcy checked the magazine of his SIG Sauer and slid the pistol into the pancake holster behind his back. He shrugged a thin plaid shirt over his T-shirt and jeans, leaving the buttons open in the front. "Do I look like a local?"

She took in his day's growth of beard and broad, muscular shoulders, the casual clothing and the baseball cap he pulled low over his forehead. "As long as you keep your mouth shut."

"I shouldn't have to speak to anyone but Lila Birdsong."

"Pretty name."

"She's an interesting lady, if her grandson's stories are anything to go by." He checked his watch. "I have to go soon."

"Are you sure you can trust this Dennison guy you called?"

"As much as I trust anyone." She could tell from his tone that he wasn't as certain about Dennison's motives for helping him as she'd hoped.

"You know the protocol for internal investigation is to use an agent's closest friends against him."

He nodded. "I'm pretty sure Dennison's the agent Quinn has assigned to keep an eye on me. So might as well let him. I have nothing to hide."

"Except me."

"Quinn already knows about you. He's already made his choice which side he's on—yours."

"How does he know I haven't gone to the dark side since we all last worked together?" she asked curiously, resting her head against the sofa cushions as she watched him pace a tight circle next to the coffee table.

"I suspect he knows more about your career than almost anyone but your supervisor." Darcy stopped in front of her, his brown eyes narrowing. "He knows more than I do, certainly."

"Do you think I've gone to the dark side?" she asked, curious.

His smile made his eyes sparkle. "I always thought you

were on the dark side, Rigsby." His smile faded. "Are you certain you're going to be all right here alone?"

She patted the holstered Glock 27 sitting on the sofa next to her. "Mr. Glock and I will be just fine."

He took the portable phone off its cradle and set it in front of her on the footlocker coffee table. "You have my cell number memorized?"

"You've spent the last hour drilling it into my brain." Her achy, tired brain. "Just go see what the witch woman has for us. And if you don't like what she has to say, you have my permission to rob a pharmacy."

"Duly noted." He opened the front door and turned to look back at her. "You sure you're okay to stay here alone?"

"I'm fine. Go. Hurry back."

She forced herself to remain upright until he was out the door. But as soon as the lock clicked shut, she slumped back against the sofa cushions, gazing at the holstered Glock by her side. It looked far away and heavy.

She hoped the next time the door opened, it would be Darcy returning. Because she was anything but fine—and in no shape to fight for her life.

LILA BIRDSONG LIVED near the top of Mulberry Rise, below the craggy face of Miller's Knob, in a small cabin surrounded by dense evergreen woods. Darcy had been there once, with Cain Dennison and a few of the other Gates agents, for a cookout in the brick barbecue pit behind Dennison's old silver Airstream trailer. From Darcy's cabin, the drive had taken five minutes.

From Hunter Bragg's cabin in the middle of nowhere, however, the winding mountain roads and sharp switchbacks took almost twenty minutes to navigate.

Twenty long minutes for something to go terribly wrong back at the cabin where McKenna waited for him to return.

Her temperature had been elevated when Darcy checked

it before he left, but not high enough for immediate concern. McKenna had downed a couple of ibuprofen and told him to go meet with Lila Birdsong, although he could tell she was skeptical that Cain Dennison's grandmother could provide anything useful to stop her wounds from becoming any more infected.

He would normally be as skeptical, but Quinn himself had consulted with Lila Birdsong about herbal remedies that could work as stopgaps in the field, when prescription medications weren't readily available.

Maybe she wouldn't be able to come up with anything to help him. But the alternative was getting antibiotics by deception or outright theft.

The road up the mountain topped off suddenly, giving Darcy a good look at the small clearing where Lila's cabin sat. The Airstream trailer that had been home to Cain Dennison was gone.

But in its place sat a Ridge County Sheriff's Department cruiser.

Chapter Four

The FBI legal attaché in Tablis, Kaziristan, had been a cramped office located at the back of the slightly shabby embassy building. Only one small window, set high in the back wall, let any natural light into the room, but the men and women who'd crowded into the tight space hadn't had much time for gazing out windows.

Eight years ago, Tablis had simmered in the harsh summer heat, close to boiling.

McKenna had been twenty-four years old, law school and twenty weeks of FBI Academy training behind her and a whole new career ahead of her. She'd been shocked and happily surprised by the assignment to the embassy legat. Even though it was largely grunt work, an embassy placement was a plum assignment for a green agent. Her superiors had assured her it was a sign that the bureau had high hopes for her career advancement.

Then everything had gone to hell in a firestorm of rocket-propelled grenades and brutal al Adar terrorists on a mission of death and chaos. She'd been lucky to get out of the embassy alive. Several other Americans hadn't fared as well, including three of her legat office associates.

She pushed herself up from the sofa, not liking the trembling weakness in her knees as she crossed to the front window to look out at the woods beyond the small cabin clearing. Morning was giving way to midday, the light moving inexorably toward the west.

Darcy had been gone almost twenty minutes.

Letting the curtains swing closed, she leaned against the windowsill, feeling achy all over. She felt hot and grimy, in desperate need of a shower and about a week of sleep, but she didn't trust her shaky limbs to hold her weight long enough to take a shower. Plus, the hot water might reopen her wounds and start the bleeding again.

Damn it.

She stumbled her way back to the sofa and sank into the cushions, hating how weak she felt. She'd worked so hard to stay fit, stay strong, keep up with the men in her FBI unit, and one stupid bullet—one that hadn't even hit any vital organs—had her as wobbly and weak as a newborn calf.

The last time she'd felt this shaky, she'd been huddled with several other embassy employees in a curtained alcove, watching an al Adar rebel named Tahir Mahmood slit the throat of one of the embassy's translators, helpless to do anything in case it alerted the other armed terrorists swarming the embassy to their hiding place.

She'd grown up just over the state line in North Carolina, until her family had moved to Raleigh when she was a teenager. Life in the Appalachian Mountains could be both beautiful and hard, and she'd experienced both sides of that life. But nothing she'd seen or heard in the hills, during her FBI training or during the first ten months of work at the US Embassy in Tablis had prepared her for the raw brutality and utter disregard for human life she'd witnessed during the embassy siege.

It had changed her. Her outlook on life. Her career goals. Her hopes.

We have to go back for him!

Her own voice rang in her mind—younger somehow, more naive and trusting than now. She'd thought they could save Michael Cameron, one of her fellow legat agents, when rockets had set their section of the damaged embassy ablaze. She'd wanted to dig through the rubble a little longer, try to reach him before the flames could, but the back section of the embassy had been crumbling around them.

Darcy had grabbed her arms and forcibly removed her from the area, hustling her, even dragging her to other parts of the embassy that had remained structurally stable during the onslaught of rocket fire.

They'd eventually met up with several other embassy employees being herded to safety by one of the embassy's Marine Security Guards, a Georgia boy named Maddox Heller. Heller had sneaked them into the alcove in the formal dining room to hide when al Adar rebels had stormed that section of the embassy.

Teresa Miles, a pretty young interpreter in her first Foreign Service assignment, hadn't been so fortunate.

A trilling sound made her nerves jangle. The phone was ringing.

She picked up the receiver and glanced at the digital display window. Darcy's cell-phone number.

Should she answer? What if something had gone wrong? What if it was a trick?

Quelling a surge of fear, she pushed the answer button and lifted the phone to her ear. But she didn't speak.

"Rigsby?" Darcy's voice was low and soft on the other end.

"Yes," she breathed. "Are you okay?"

"For the moment." Even over the phone, she could hear the tension in his voice. "When I arrived at Lila Birdsong's cabin, there was a sheriff's cruiser there. I think I know who it is, but she knows me. I can't risk going inside yet until she comes out."

"Won't she see the Land Rover?"

"Not unless she's looking. I've hidden in the woods off the road."

"Darcy, this is crazy. Just get back here. We'll figure out something else. I'm feeling better already," she added, wondering if he could discern the lie on his end of the line.

"No, you're not," he growled, answering her question. "I've been searching the internet on my phone while waiting, and I encountered some options for us to try before we start breaking into pharmacies."

"Don't take any stupid risks, Darcy."

She could almost hear his smile. "I never take stupid risks, Rigsby. Only smart ones. I'll be in touch." He hung up before she could respond.

She hung up and set the phone on the coffee table, her hand trembling and her pulse pounding in her ears.

THE SHERIFF'S CRUISER passed slowly on its way down the mountain road, the midday sun glinting off the chrome and briefly obscuring the driver as the vehicle approached Darcy's hiding place in the woods. He'd left the SUV behind and walked closer to the road for a better view.

The glint faded as the cruiser rolled past, giving Darcy a good view of the driver's shoulder-length bob of dark hair and pretty profile. Sara Lindsey. Cain Dennison's girlfriend.

Darcy knew that Sara and Cain's grandmother had become close a few months earlier, when Sara had returned home to Ridge County after several years as a Birmingham, Alabama, police officer. Maybe her visit to Lila Birdsong had been entirely unrelated to the call he'd made to Cain Dennison.

Or maybe it had everything to do with it.

He pulled out his phone and punched in Dennison's phone number. The Gates agent answered on the third ring. "Darcy?"

"Did you tell anyone besides your grandmother that I was going to visit her?"

"No." Cain sounded curious. "Did something happen?"

"Your girlfriend was at your grandmother's place when I arrived."

"So?"

"So, I didn't expect to see a Ridge County sheriff's deputy as part of the welcoming committee."

Cain sounded confused. "It's not like you don't know Sara, Darcy. You're a friend, not a suspect."

On the contrary, Darcy realized with a gut-twisting wrench. He didn't have any friends. He couldn't afford them.

Not with McKenna Rigsby's life hanging in the balance.

THE RATTLE OF the doorknob sent a hard shudder down McKenna's back. Groping for the Glock, she knocked the pistol and holster to the floor.

Damn it!

The thought of bending down to pick up the fallen weapon was almost more than she could contemplate, but she forced herself into motion, retrieving the holster, grabbing the grip of the pistol and sliding it out smoothly just as the cabin door swung open.

Darcy froze in the doorway, raising his hands, one of which held a large plastic sack. "It's me. Don't shoot."

She lowered the pistol, her hands shaking. "You could have called to warn me."

"I thought you might be sleeping. You need rest, and I didn't want to risk waking you." He locked the door behind him and looked around the room. "Have you been here the whole time I was gone?"

"I took a bathroom break about thirty minutes ago." She didn't tell him that walking down the short hallway to the bathroom had sapped most of her strength. Nodding at the plastic bag, she asked, "What's that?"

"Some things I found at the compounding pharmacy in town."

"So you didn't make it to see the witch woman."

"Nope. Didn't think the risk was worth it." He sat in the armchair across from her and emptied the bag onto the foot-locker between them. "This is something called Dragon's Blood. Tree sap of some sort. Said to have strong antibiotic, antiviral and antifungal properties. Plus, anti-inflammatory and analgesic."

"Overachiever," she muttered, eyeing the dark red liquid in the small bottle with skepticism. "Does it do windows, too?"

Darcy's lips quirked as he pushed another small bottle toward her. "Eucalyptus oil. Also supposed to be antibiotic, if the articles on the internet are anything to go by."

"Because everything you read on the internet is true."

He slanted another amused look at her. "This is good old fashioned aloe vera gel. I figure it can't hurt."

"And that?" she asked, pointing at the bottle that sat behind the rest.

"Betadine. If hospitals use it, it must be effective, yes?"

"Works for me." She leaned forward to pick up the bottle of Betadine and gasped at the burning ache in her side. "Ow."

Darcy was up from the chair and by her side in a second. "Sit back. You're doing too much."

To her horror, hot tears stung her eyes. She blinked them back. "I'm fine."

"You're far from fine. You're injured and probably haven't had a good night's sleep in days. Have you?"

"What I'd really like is a shower," she blurted before she could think better of it.

"That can be arranged." Darcy's dark eyes met hers.

Despite the pain in her side, despite the weakness in her limbs, she felt a flood of pure sexual heat flow between them, and her breath stilled in her lungs. The intensity of his regard overwhelmed her, but she couldn't drag her gaze away.

He broke the connection first, moving away and turning his attention to the bottles sitting on the coffee table. "A bath might be the better option."

He was right about that. Her legs would never hold her upright long enough to finish a shower. "That would be lovely."

"Stay right here." As he passed her on the way to the bathroom, he brushed the back of his hand briefly against her cheek. As much as she might have wanted to believe it was a simple show of affection, she had a feeling he'd been surreptitiously checking her for fever.

"Am I burning up?" she called after him.

"Didn't even singe my fingers," he called back, his tone light. But she heard worry lurking just beneath the surface.

She'd been running around in the woods for six hours, forced to ignore her pain and weakness. The wounds had remained untreated, open to any sort of airborne pathogens that might have found their way to the bloody holes in her side.

She'd spent a lot of time zigzagging to throw off her pursuers, and for what? They'd still spotted her less than a mile from Nick Darcy's cabin. She'd still had to run for her life.

Darcy came back a few minutes later. "Your bath is ready," he intoned in his plummiest accent.

He watched with hawk-like intensity as she gingerly inched her way toward him, though he kept his hands to himself, letting her pull her own weight, as if he sensed that she needed to make that small, unconvincing show of strength.

In the warm, cozy bathroom, the fragrant air smelled

like crisp green apples. She turned in the doorway to look at Darcy. "Green apple is Susie's favorite."

He smiled, his eyes crinkling at the corners. "Explains why Bragg always smells so nice."

Steam rose from the foamy bathwater. "I think I can take it from here."

"Call out if you need me." With a long, narrow-eyed gaze that sent a shiver skittering down her back, Darcy backed out of the bathroom and closed the door behind him.

She stripped off the borrowed T-shirt and, gritting her teeth, tugged the bandages away from her bullet wounds. Using the small oval mirror over the pedestal sink, she took a look at the injury. There was distinct redness and inflammation around the entry and exit wounds, but she didn't see signs that infection had spread. That was good, wasn't it?

After she finished undressing, she headed over to the tub. She had to grip the sides of the tub to keep from falling over as she stepped into the bubble bath. The water was deliciously hot against her skin, and for a second, she thought the bath might turn out to be more enjoyable than she expected.

Then the water hit her wounds, and she couldn't hold back a sharp yelp.

A couple of seconds later, the bathroom door slammed open and Darcy filled the doorway, his dark eyes alert.

She ducked down until the foamy water covered her naked breasts, shooting him a baleful look.

The concerned expression faded into a ridiculous smirk. "Hot water hit the wounds?"

"Yes, as a matter of fact."

"Are you all right?"

She nodded.

"I can stay in here. In case you need help." His lips curved a little more, and for a second, she was tempted to splash water on him. Then it occurred to her what he was doing. He was trying to distract her from the pain still slicing through her ravaged side.

"I'm fine," she assured him. "Really, I am. Not pretending to be stronger than I am."

"Are you certain you want me to leave?"

"Positive," she answered, mocking his accent.

His quirked lips made it all the way to a smile. "I'm told I'm excellent at scrubbing backs."

"I'm sure you are. But I think I can reach my own back." She almost believed she could, although she wasn't in a hurry to test the theory.

"You know, maybe we should consider conserving water, since we're borrowing the place from someone else—" He reached for the top button of his shirt.

"Out, Darcy."

He dropped his hands and grinned. "Call if you change your mind."

"I won't," she vowed as he headed out of the bathroom again.

At least, she hoped she wouldn't. The mental image of Nick Darcy's big, soapy hands moving over her body was already making her feel weak.

And weak was the last thing she needed to be around him.

ABOUT TWO MINUTES before Darcy was ready to barge back into the bathroom to see what was taking so long, McKenna emerged wrapped in a fluffy terry-cloth robe. "I found this in the bathroom. Must belong to Susie."

"Right."

"Kind of hoping she has more clothes around here. She's a little taller than I am, but we wear close to the same size." She tugged the garment more tightly around her. He saw a spot of blood beginning to appear and spread on the side of the robe.

He rose quickly to reach her. "You're bleeding again."

She looked down at the bloodstain. "Oh. I don't think it's a lot." But as she looked back up at him, she began to sway a little, her eyes drifting unfocused.

He scooped her up and carried her back to the bedroom, depositing her on the bed. Her hands dropped away from the lapels of the robe as her eyes struggled to focus, and the robe gaped open, revealing the shadowy curves of her breasts. They were milky pale, one apricot-colored nipple just visible under the edge of the lapel.

Desire lanced through him, but he quelled it ruthlessly, tugging the edges of the robe closed before he realized he needed to remove the robe entirely if he wanted to take a look at her wounds.

"I'm okay," she murmured, sounding anything but.

He checked her pulse and found it fast and a little weak. Her skin felt dry and loose. "Rigsby, did you drink any water while I was gone?"

"I ran out, and I didn't feel like getting up to get more."

"Damn it, Rigsby, you're dehydrated. We must get some fluids into you before you pass out." He brushed her hair away from her face, not liking how warm she was. Maybe the hot bath had been a bad idea.

He crossed to the closet door and pulled it open, hoping he'd find some of Susannah Marsh's clothes hanging there, but there were very few hanging clothes, only a couple of jackets and what looked like an Army dress uniform stored in a plastic garment bag.

"Try the drawers," McKenna suggested, her words weak and slurred.

He hit pay dirt in the dresser at the foot of the bed. Two drawers contained women's underwear and a variety of shorts, jeans and T-shirts.

"She likes to dress down these days." McKenna had pushed herself up on her elbows and was looking at him through a tangle of ginger curls. "She can be herself here, again. She was always a tomboy. Hated heels and skirts and all that girlie stuff, as she calls it."

"She's gone blond-haired and blue-eyed again."

"I know." McKenna's eyes followed him as he returned to the bed with a bra, panties, a light blue T-shirt and a pair of navy running shorts. They were a murky green color at the moment, like a mountain pool. "You gonna dress me, Darcy?"

"Don't tempt me," he murmured, handing over the clothing. "I'll be in the kitchen getting you something to eat and refilling your water bottle. Call me if you need me."

He took several deep, bracing breaths as he refilled the water bottle, adding a little ice this time in hopes of helping her fight the fever. It was utterly ridiculous that he found himself thinking of stripping her naked now, of all times, considering her weakened condition.

But she'd always had that effect on him, hadn't she? Even in the high-stress atmosphere of the US Embassy in Tablis, McKenna Rigsby had been a constant temptation to him.

It wasn't just that she was beautiful in that fresh-faced, natural way of hers. It was also her sharp mind, her blazing intellect and her dogged determination to reach her goal in any situation, despite any obstacle.

He might have saved her from sacrificing her life in a lost cause to save her colleague that fateful day in Tablis, but she'd saved him first, dragging his concussed and woozy ass back inside the embassy before the terrorists blew up the gates and surged inside.

As he set the water bottle on the table, he heard the sound of footsteps behind him, moving at a quick but unsteady pace. He turned to find McKenna standing in the kitchen doorway, her face sickly white. She'd managed to put on the T-shirt, but she wore only panties beneath, and blood was trickling down her left leg.

As he took a step toward her, she grabbed his arm, her green eyes wide with fear.

"What is it?" he asked, his gut tightening with alarm.

Her voice came out in a raspy whisper. "Someone's outside."

Chapter Five

He was so warm. So solid. Right now, McKenna felt like a mass of cold jelly, shivering and wobbling as she followed Darcy back to the bedroom. He turned suddenly, catching her as she stumbled into him and easing her onto the foot of the bed. "Stay right there. I need to find you something a little warmer to wear."

Resisting the temptation to drop back onto the soft mattress, she watched him search the dresser drawers until he found a pair of jeans. "May be a little long for you, but we'll have to make do. Can you get them on?"

It was going to be hell wriggling into jeans, she realized, but she took the pants from him and did her best, biting back a deep groan.

He moved to the window and took a quick peek out the curtains. "Nobody's there."

"I swear, there was."

"I don't doubt you." He left the window and crossed to where she sat. "Do you need help?"

She could tell from the impatient tone of his voice that he didn't want to be slowed down by having to aid her in dressing herself, so she shook her head. "Do whatever you need to do."

He touched her face briefly, his fingers cold against her

skin. His brow furrowed as he dropped his hand away. "I'll be right back."

She finished tugging the jeans over her hips and slumped back on the bed, feeling as if she'd just run a marathon. She was still sitting in that position when Darcy returned a few minutes later with a large backpack and a medium-size duffel, both olive drab and well used. "I've packed supplies in the backpack," he told her, setting it on the floor by her feet. "Food, water, flashlights and tools. In case we have to bug out."

"How can we bug out?" she asked. "If someone's out there, they already know we're here."

"There's another way out," he said cryptically as he held his hand out to her. "Let's get those pants zipped and see if we can find you some socks and a jacket."

She let him pull her to her feet, not even protesting when he caught the tab of her zipper and pulled it up to close the fly of the jeans. But the slight curve of his lips as he snapped the button closed on the waistband sent a flood of heat pouring straight to her core. "That's rather the opposite of what I'm used to," he murmured.

A flare of jealousy snaked through her, catching her off guard. "How used to it are you?" she asked before she could stop herself.

His dark eyes snapped up to meet hers, a hint of humor dancing in their depths. "Gentlemen never unzip and tell."

"Tease," she murmured, dropping back to the edge of the bed while he went in search of socks.

He found a pair and brought them over to her, bending to put them on her feet.

"I can do it," she protested.

"I'm sure you can, but there's no point in your expending any extra energy. If we have to leave, you'll need all the strength you can muster." He slipped the second sock on her other foot and reached for the shoes she'd been wearing that morning when she showed up at his door. They were a sturdy pair of cross trainers, built for support, and they'd probably helped keep her going long after her stamina had begun to fail her.

Right now, however, they felt like two stone blocks tied to her feet. She wasn't sure how she was going to walk across the room, much less go on the run.

As Darcy turned back to the bed holding a corduroy jacket that clearly belonged to her cousin, a rapping sound came from the front of the house, and they both froze, staring at each other.

"Not a sound," he murmured, touching his hand to her face. "Stay put."

Then he turned and was gone.

She heard his footsteps all the way down the uncarpeted hall, then moving across the front room. The door opened, and she heard the soft murmur of voices. Then, with a click, the door closed again, and the cabin fell silent.

What was going on? The curiosity that had been a characteristic part of her life since she was a tiny child kicked in with ferocity, tempting her to ignore Darcy's order to stay put.

But her weary, aching body wouldn't comply with her mental order to start moving. She felt as weak as a newborn kitten, and just about as useful.

To her dismay, she started to cry.

"WHAT THE HELL are you doing here?" Cain Dennison's gray eyes narrowed as Darcy hustled him out of the doorway and back onto the porch.

"Checking on the place for Bragg," Darcy lied. "What are you doing here, following me?"

Dennison raked his fingers through his dark hair, looking suspicious. "You didn't show up at my grandmother's place earlier."

"Yeah, changed my mind."

"Why?"

Darcy ignored the question. "How did you know to look for me here?"

"Your vehicle's still fitted with a company GPS tracker." Dennison arched one dark eyebrow. "Why'd you change your mind?"

"I found what I wanted to know on the internet."

"What did you want to know?"

Darcy crossed his arms, noting his fellow agent's sudden inquisitiveness. Cain Dennison had never been the talkative sort, and while Darcy considered him one of his closer friends at The Gates, it was more a matter of his not really having any close friends to speak of. He'd grown up in the spotlight as the son of an American ambassador, and his parents had drilled into him warnings about the folly of letting down one's guard to the wrong people.

What they'd failed to teach him was how to tell the wrong people from the right people. So he'd ended up trusting almost no one at all.

"Research for a book," he answered. "Since I'm not allowed to work for my pay, I thought I should start doing something constructive."

"And you're doing it here at Bragg's primitive cabin?"

"Was your only purpose in tracking me down to ask me why I didn't show up at your grandmother's place? Because I've answered that question."

"Are you sure it wasn't because you got there and saw Sara's cruiser?"

Darcy grimaced. "You were assigned to watch me, weren't you?"

For a moment, he thought Dennison wasn't going to answer. Then the other agent gave a brief nod. "Yes."

"Quinn seriously believes I'm the mole at the agency?" He shouldn't have felt hurt, but he did, he realized. While

Darcy might not have many close friends, Alexander Quinn was one of the few people in the world he'd come to trust—for the most part. He certainly trusted Quinn to do what he thought was the right thing for the most people involved, at least.

But clearly, Quinn didn't return that trust.

"I don't think he does," Dennison said quietly. "I know I don't. You don't have that sort of treachery in you."

"You don't really know me, Dennison."

"I guess not. Because you're lying to my face right now, and I sure didn't expect that of you."

Guilt pricked Darcy's conscience, but it wasn't just his own life at stake. McKenna Rigsby was waiting inside, ill and feverish, entirely dependent on his ability to protect her. His loyalty to Cain Dennison, to Alexander Quinn and The Gates, had to come second to her.

She was relying on him. He couldn't let her down.

"Is there anything else you need?" he asked Dennison in a cool, imperious tone he'd learned from his father.

Dennison's eyes widened slightly and he took a step back. "No. I don't need a damn thing from you." He turned and descended the porch stairs.

Darcy was tempted to call him back, but he quelled the urge and watched until Dennison had disappeared into the woods. He took a deep breath, filling his lungs with cool mountain air, then turned and went back inside the cabin.

He found McKenna sitting where he'd left her, slumped forward with her chin on her chest. "He's gone."

She lifted her head slowly, and the look of sheer misery on her tearstained face made his breath catch. "For how long?"

He crouched in front of her. "What's wrong?" He caught her face between his hands, alarmed at how hot she was. "You're burning up."

"I don't feel so great."

"Let me see your wounds." He tugged gently at the hem of the T-shirt to expose her open wounds. Though the entry and exit wounds were puffy and red, he'd seen worse, he realized with relief. But if the infection was strong enough to cause McKenna to run a fever, it was still a source of concern.

"We need to clean your wounds out and get some of these treatments started," he told her in a firm tone.

"No, please. I can't take it right now."

Her teeth were chattering, he saw with alarm. Was her fever increasing?

"Rigsby, you have to." He crouched in front of her, taking her hands. Her fingers were icy cold; he rubbed gently to warm them. "I know you're tired and you're hurting, but we may need to leave here, sooner or later."

"Who was at the door?"

"One of my colleagues." He told her about Dennison's visit as he continued to warm her hands between his. "I think he suspects I'm up to something strange."

"You told him you were checking on the place for Hunter?"

"Yes, but I don't think he believes me."

"What do you think he'll do?" Her teeth had stopped chattering, he noticed, and her eyes seemed a little clearer than before.

"Nothing for now," he answered. "Possibly report my presence here to Alexander Quinn."

"Is that good or bad?"

He thought about the question for a moment. "Neutral, I suppose. He's not going to interfere as long as we're safe."

"Are we?" she asked quietly as he released her hands and started to rise. "Safe, I mean."

He cupped her hot cheek with his palm. "As much as we can hope to be at the moment." He dropped his hand away and opened his backpack to retrieve the first-aid kit he'd packed in case they needed to evacuate quickly.

Feeling her gaze on him, he turned to look at her. The tears were back, trembling on her lower lashes. "I'm sorry."

He made himself look away, knowing pity was the last thing she wanted. "For getting shot? I doubt you chose that option willingly."

"For going weak-kneed on you."

"That's the infection and dehydration. Speaking of that—" He reached in the backpack and pulled out a bottle of water. He twisted the cap open and handed the bottle to her. "Drink up."

She did as he asked, blinking back the tears that had formed in her eyes, not letting them fall. This was the McKenna Rigsby he remembered, the tough, gutsy redhead who'd taken the US Embassy in Tablis by storm. "Hurricane Rigsby," some of the guys in security had called her, for she'd had a way of blowing into a room and blowing out again, leaving everything and everyone upended behind her.

He finished gathering the supplies he needed and carried everything to the bed where she sat. "Do people still call you Hurricane?" he asked as he lifted the hem of her T-shirt again to check her injury.

"Not to my face," she said bluntly, flashing him a pained smile.

He smiled back. "No, never to your face."

"I'm not the same person, Darcy." Her voice darkened. "A lot has happened since I walked into the embassy almost nine years ago."

"A lot happened in the time you were there."

"No kidding."

He poured Betadine onto a cotton ball and pressed it to the entry wound, eliciting a soft hiss from her lips. "Sorry."

"Don't dally."

"Wouldn't dream of it." He applied the antiseptic liberally to both wounds and the skin surrounding them. "Do you stay in touch with anyone from the Tablis legat?"

"No." She grimaced as he dabbed the excess Betadine with a clean cloth. "I don't think many of us wanted reminders."

"Is that why you never answered my calls?"

Her gaze flicked up to meet his. "Mostly."

"Mostly?" He applied aloe vera gel to the wounds, taking care to be gentle.

"My reasons for not responding to your calls were complicated."

"Meaning, you were still furious at me but didn't want to have to admit it?" He tried to keep his tone light, but the words he uttered stung, even coming from his own lips. "You clearly haven't forgiven me for what happened to Michael Cameron."

She shook her head. "I haven't forgiven myself."

"For listening to me?"

"For not figuring out a way to get to him before the fire did." A hard shudder rippled through her body. "They drummed it into us, over and over—know the layout. Know where the exits are, where the escape routes lie. And I should have known the place better, figured out another way to get to him—"

He wiped his hands on a towel. "There was no other way, Rigsby."

McKenna shook her head. "There had to be."

"There wasn't. If there had been, I'd have taken a chance on trying to get him out of there." He put his hands on her upper arms, forcing her to look at him again. "I did have the layout memorized. Completely. Backward and forward. The problem was, the wall took a direct hit. It blocked any outlet entirely. It would have taken heavy equipment to dig Cameron out, sweetheart. But there wasn't enough time."

She bent forward, and for a moment, he thought she was about to lose consciousness. But she pressed her forehead against his, lifting her hands to cradle his face. "Promise me that's the truth?"

He closed his hands over hers. "I promise."

She pulled back, gently tugging her hands away. Leaning sideways, she pulled her T-shirt hem up again. "Let's get this over with."

He bandaged her wounds as quickly as he could and put the excess supplies back into the first-aid kit. He pulled out a packet of ibuprofen and ripped it open. "Need more water?"

She looked at the empty bottle of water she'd set beside her on the bed. "I guess I need to get more fluids in me."

"You'll feel better if you do," he assured her, pulling a second bottle of water from the backpack and opening it for her. "Take these ibuprofen. It will relieve your pain and bring down your fever."

She took the tablets, washing them down with a long swig of water. "Be honest, Darcy. How badly infected are my wounds?"

"They're infected," he admitted, "but I've seen much worse. You're in good health otherwise, aren't you?"

She nodded.

"And we've been aggressive about cleaning out the wounds and treating them. What you need most is to get fully rehydrated and get some rest." He stood up. "I don't think we need to go on the run again quite yet."

"What about the visit from your friend?"

"He's suspicious, but Quinn will keep him from going off half-cocked," Darcy replied, wishing he felt a little more confident. "I'll worry about Dennison. You worry about getting some sleep. Would you like another cup of soup before you rest?"

She shook her head, her tangled curls dancing around

her face like living things. "I just want to sleep for about a week."

"You can sleep as much as you want." He couldn't resist wrapping one of those coppery curls around his finger.

She looked up at him, her eyes liquid and as dark as the dusk falling outside the bedroom window, only a faint rim of green showing. "Where are you going to sleep?"

The question was innocent, but he couldn't stop his body's quick, fierce reaction. He tugged his hand from her hair. "I'll be on the sofa. Call out if you need me. I'm a light sleeper."

She caught his hand as he turned to go, her fingers no longer cold. The heat of her touch burned all the way to his core. "Darcy, thank you. For everything. I know this can't be much fun for you."

"On the contrary," he said, entirely sincere. "I've been bored senseless for the past week. A rogue FBI agent falling wounded on my doorstep? I can hardly contain my excitement. So, no, Agent Rigsby. Thank *you*."

As he'd intended, she smiled. "Anytime, Darcy."

In the hall closet, he found a blanket and an extra pillow, to his relief. He might not have turned out quite as pampered and privileged as his parents had reared him to be, but he liked his creature comforts as much as the next man, particularly when he knew he might have to rough it soon enough. At any moment, they might have to run for their lives.

He knew Cain Dennison wouldn't be a problem. Quinn would make certain of it. But someone was out there, looking for McKenna. Maybe several someones.

And until they figured out exactly who and why, they remained in grave danger.

Chapter Six

The wound on Nick Darcy's forehead had finally stopped bleeding, but the previously unstanched flow had made a mess of his face and the front of his formerly snowy-white shirt. McKenna had gotten him as far as the embassy ballroom before he stopped short and looked around him as if trying to make sense of the chaos.

The staccato cadence of gunfire, punctuated now and then by booming rocket blasts, couldn't drown out the cries of fear and pain that echoed through the embassy halls.

"Darcy?" She spoke in a whisper, but the sound seemed harsh and loud to her ears.

His unfocused gaze slid toward her but didn't quite connect. "The ambassador—"

"Can't be helped now." She caught his hand in hers, ignoring the sticky warmth of his blood against her palm. At least he was alive. They were both alive. So many others weren't. They'd already passed three dead embassy employees to get this far. "Darcy, we have to find a way out."

"No way out," he murmured.

"I know there's an underground exit. I've heard people talk about it. We just have to find it."

"It's beneath the west wing." His gaze met hers, finally focused. "It's covered with rubble. We can't get to it."

Her heart skipped a beat. "So we're trapped?"

His fingers tightened around hers. "I didn't say that. We simply must think our way through this." He lifted his free hand to his forehead, wincing as he touched the bloody lump the flying shrapnel had left over his right eye. "Unfortunately, thinking isn't coming easily to me at the moment."

"That's why you have me." She tugged his hand, moving toward the ballroom exit. This area was too exposed, too easy a target for the rebels. "Let's find a place to hunker down and think."

He didn't resist, following her from the ballroom into the narrow corridor that led toward the events kitchen. Once there, they found three of the embassy food staff huddled in the corner. One of them rose at the sound of their footsteps, brandishing a large meat cleaver. It was Jamil Guram, she saw, the embassy's sous chef from Punjab—the one in India, he was always quick to specify, not Pakistan. His dark eyes locked with hers and the cleaver clattered to the floor. "Agent Rigsby," he breathed.

"Just the three of you?" she asked.

"Yes," he answered in his lightly accented English. "Will you be able to get us out of here? The terrorists are not far away. I have heard them shouting nearby."

She couldn't promise him anything, she realized with dismay. She wasn't sure any of them would get out of here alive.

Behind her, she felt Darcy move closer to her, the heat of his body spreading across her back, seeming to imbue her with added strength. She straightened her spine. "We'll do our best," she promised Jamil.

But before the final word escaped her tongue, hell descended in a roar of fire and brimstone.

McKenna sat up with a gasp, her ragged breath loud in the darkness, joining the cacophony of her hammering pulse and the throbbing agony in her side. She was surrounded by darkness so deep and impenetrable that she thought for a moment she was still dreaming.

Then, as her eyes began to adjust to the gloom, she made out the shapes of ordinary things—a dresser, a closet door, a window where the faintest of ambient light trickled past the barrier of curtains.

She was holed up in Hunter Bragg's cabin in the Smokies, she remembered, her pulse still racing. She had been shot by someone in the woods, someone in cahoots with one of her FBI colleagues.

And Nick Darcy was sleeping on the sofa in the front room, playing the role of her protector after eight years of silence and distance between them.

She slumped back against the pillows.

Why had she really come here? Was it what she'd told Darcy—that he was the only person in the area she felt she could trust? She supposed there was some truth in that statement, but it wasn't the whole truth, was it?

She'd come to him because she'd been afraid she might be dying. And she wanted to see him again, one more time.

He was so not her type. If her high school friends had been around at the embassy in Tablis, they'd have been shocked if she'd admitted to finding buttoned-up, very formal Nick Darcy attractive. Her tastes had always run more toward the sweet-talking, hard-living country boys she'd grown up with, all brazen flash and Southern charm.

Darcy was nothing like those guys, but still, there had been something about him, some dangerous gleam in his dark eyes, that had piqued her curiosity and made her want to know him better.

And then his quiet competence and courtly manners had sucked her in completely, even though he was so off-limits to her it wasn't funny. Their relationship—if you could even call it that—had been carried out in lingering gazes and furtive touches, stolen conversations and one near kiss that had left her aching for days.

She knew he'd grown up in London for the first eighteen years of his life, with the occasional summer in his father's native Virginia. His mother was a British citizen, a lesser peer whose name had once been bandied about as a potential bride for the royal family—a fact that had been a source of amusement to Darcy, who described his mother as a down-to-earth horsewoman better suited for hunts than balls.

"My mother's rustic leanings used to drive my father crazy," he'd shared over a quick lunch one day in the embassy kitchen. "Until he figured out that she knew where all the skeletons were hidden because of all that time she'd spent as a girl, wandering about on the country estates of some of England's most influential parliamentarians."

That he loved his mother had been obvious. That he'd respected his father had been equally clear. What had most intrigued McKenna, however, was how distanced he seemed to feel from both of them.

"You're awake."

The sound of Darcy's voice in the dark sent a delicious shiver sliding down her spine. She turned her head to find his dark silhouette in the bedroom's open doorway.

"Just woke." Her voice sounded raspy. She cleared her throat and spoke again. "What time is it?"

"A little after midnight. Time for you to take some more ibuprofen." He flicked the switch on the wall and light flooded the room, nearly blinding her. "Sorry."

Her eyes adjusted quickly to the brightness, quickly enough that she could enjoy the sight of Darcy's slow, long-limbed approach to the bed. Barefoot, wearing a pair of worn jeans and a rumpled gray T-shirt, his hair mussed and longer than she remembered from his time at the embassy,

Darcy looked a hell of a lot more like one of those redneck boys she'd always favored than he ever had before.

But when he sat beside her and spoke, the illusion disappeared, and the cool, competent former DSS agent she'd known in Tablis reappeared. "I thought I heard you call out."

She tried to remember her dream, but it was a tangle of images and snippets of memory she couldn't seem to make cohere. "I think I was dreaming about Tablis," she murmured as he pressed the back of his hand to her cheek, then her forehead.

"Your fever seems to have subsided." He reached down and pulled his backpack onto the bed beside him. "Let's check your temperature."

She caught his hand as he started to unzip the bag. "I know you made the right decision in Tablis. I do."

His dark eyes lifted to meet hers. "I wasn't going to let you get killed for nothing. And without heavy equipment and a full extraction crew, we weren't going to get Cameron out of there."

"I lost my head. So much death—"

He brushed his fingertip against her cheek, and she felt the wetness of tears she hadn't been aware of spilling. "You were brave. And strong. I wouldn't have survived the siege without you."

"Back at ya," she murmured.

He pressed the temporal artery thermometer against her temple and waited for the beep. "Ninety-eight point eight," he murmured. "That's good."

"I feel better," she admitted.

"Also good." He shook two ibuprofen tablets from the plastic bottle and handed them to her. "Finish off that water washing these down and I'll get you a fresh bottle."

She did as he asked and handed over the empty bottle. "Have you gotten any sleep?"

"Some."

She wasn't sure she believed him. "Don't make yourself sick trying to take care of me. I'm better already, I promise."

"I'm fine," he insisted.

"Is the sofa uncomfortable? Maybe you should be in the bed—"

His eyebrows ticked upward. "You want to share?"

His tone was light, but the look in his eyes was sultry and serious, and despite her still-weakened condition, despite eight years of separation and a million very good reasons why giving in to lust was a bad idea, she was sorely tempted to call his bluff.

She managed to resist. "I could take the sofa."

He made a face. "That's no fun."

"Seriously, Darcy. I'm feeling better, and I've slept on so many office sofas so many times I've lost count. Bragg's sofa can't be worse than those."

"It's not. It's quite comfortable. Truly."

He seemed sincere, and now that she'd found a position on the bed that seemed to be mostly pain-free, she wasn't in a hurry to change her accommodations. So she didn't argue further. "Any more unwanted visitors? Threatening phone calls from the boss?"

He shook his head. "Silent as the tomb."

She winced. "Lovely metaphor."

"Simile," he corrected with a twitch of his lips.

"Still an insufferable grammar scold, I see." She softened her words with a smile.

"It's part of my charm."

Her smile widened. "Sadly, it's most of your charm."

He laughed. "I see some things haven't changed in eight years. You can still smart off with the best of them."

"Lots of practice, working for the government." Before she could quell the urge, she caught his hand in hers. "I was surprised to hear you'd left the DSS. I thought you'd be a lifer."

Looking down at their hands, he curled his fingers over hers, his thumb rubbing lightly against the back of her hand. "After the siege, a lot of things changed for me."

"You stayed on for seven more years."

He nodded. "I did."

"But your heart wasn't in it?"

He grimaced. "It wasn't that, exactly."

"Then what was it?"

He let go of her hand and stood up. "Let's table any long stories until we both get some sleep."

"Darcy—"

"We'll talk in the morning." He left quickly, closing the door behind him.

She slumped back against her pillows, frustrated. He'd always been careful and self-protective, she remembered, and if anything, the passing years had made him more so.

But she needed to know she could trust him. And how could she trust him if he was hiding things from her?

DARCY WOKE TO light filtering through the curtains of the front windows. Rubbing his bleary eyes, he checked his watch. Almost seven. He'd overslept.

Grimacing at the ache in his back from a night on the unfamiliar sofa, he pushed to a sitting position and stretched his arms and legs, trying to get some of the kinks out.

"Good morning."

McKenna's voice, close behind him, gave him a start. He twisted to look at her and found her looking surprisingly alert, considering how weak she'd been by the time he'd tucked her into bed. "You look better."

Her lips curved just short of a smile. "I feel a lot better."

"That could change quickly," he warned as he rose and

turned to face her. "You hungry? I think we can come up with something from the pantry."

"Yeah, I've already been scoping it out. There's frozen waffles in the freezer and some syrup and peanut butter in the pantry."

He grimaced.

"You'd prefer kippers, I suppose, Prince Charles?"

"Not a Brit."

That time her lips made it all the way to a smile. "Good, because we're fresh out of kippers."

He followed her to the kitchen and waved at the small table by the window. "You sit. I'll see what our options are."

"I'm telling you, I looked. No milk or eggs. Just a few frozen things and nonperishables." She sat at the table and watched while he poked through the cabinets and refrigerator for a few moments before having to concede she was right.

"I could run into town later for supplies," he said.

She looked up sharply. "What if you're followed back here?"

"Would you rather starve?" His words came out more sharply than he'd intended, thanks to his edgy nerves.

She slumped in her chair. "I shouldn't have gone to your cabin in the first place. I knew it might put you in danger."

He felt a sharp stab of guilt as he closed the refrigerator door. "I'm glad you did. You couldn't have gone on much longer with those wounds untreated."

"But you would be back at your cabin, not breaking and entering and avoiding your colleagues."

He crossed to her, crouching in front of her chair. "Stop, Rigsby. If you hadn't shown up when you did, I'd still be fuming about my suspension and feeling sorry for myself. I needed the distraction."

One corner of her lips curved. "I live to be a distraction."

He barely kept himself from pushing back the auburn

curls that had fallen to frame her face. "You're quite good at it, you know." He pushed to his feet. "Waffles?"

"With peanut butter and syrup," she said, her tone brighter.

He grimaced again. "Hillbilly."

"Not a hillbilly," she retorted with a grin.

As he struggled against an answering smile, heat coiled low in his abdomen, reminding him that friendship with McKenna Rigsby might be more dangerous than conflict.

He found a jar of strawberry preserves in the refrigerator and spread the treacly berries over his toasted waffle, while McKenna slathered peanut butter and syrup over her own. She ate with a gusto that made him feel hopeful that they'd managed to turn the tide of her infection.

She seemed stronger and clearer-eyed, as well, when she helped him wash and dry their plates and put them away. "You weren't lying about feeling better, were you?" he asked as he took the dishrag from her hands and folded it.

Taking a step closer, she took the dishrag from his hands and set it on the counter. Heat from her body swept over him like a wave, setting off tremors low in his abdomen. "Maybe you missed your calling, Darcy. Although your bedside manner could use a little help."

He took a step back before realizing he was trapped against the counter.

McKenna's eyebrows arched a notch. "Last night, you said we'd talk this morning. Well, it's morning, Darcy. So talk."

"I could ask the same of you, Rigsby." He pushed away from the counter, closing the space between them to inches. "You told me a little about what you've been doing, but you know what you haven't told me? What you did to make the FBI put out an APB on you."

She sighed and took a step backward, bumping into one of the kitchen chairs. She reached back to steady herself before lifting her chin and meeting his gaze. "I ignored a direct order from my SAC."

He frowned. Special Agents in Charge, or SACs, were direct superiors in the FBI chain of command. If her SAC had given her an order, disobeying it was a big violation of the rules. "Why?"

"Because he told me to meet another agent at a staging point for extraction."

"He wanted you to bug out."

"He wanted me to meet someone I had reason to believe might want me dead." Her clear green eyes met his steadily. "I overheard a discussion between a man named Calvin Hopkins and an anarchist who goes by the name Komodo. Don't ask—I have no idea why he goes by that name. But Hopkins told Komodo that he'd gotten a tip from the Fibber."

He frowned. "Komodo and the Fibber? Sounds like a comic book."

She took a step toward him again, and the fierce look in her eyes sent him backward again until his hips hit the edge of the counter. "It may sound comical to you, but the Fibber, as they called him, is apparently someone in the FBI, because he blew my cover completely. I barely got off the BRI compound without being caught. Then I got the call from my boss to meet an agent named Cade Landry for extraction."

"And you don't trust Landry?"

"I don't trust anyone!" Her voice rose with frustration. "Not a damned person in the FBI or anywhere else." She took a deep breath and lowered her voice. "I want to trust you, Darcy. I need to trust you."

"You can," he said.

Her gaze searched his, looking for God only knew what. Some secret sign that he was worthy of her faith, he supposed. He didn't know how to reassure her. Either she believed in him or she didn't.

"Okay. I believe you." Her lips curved and she took a step closer, placing her hands on his shoulders. She smelled good, the scent of green-apple bubble bath lingering on her skin. "Thank you. For the way you've taken care of me. And for believing me."

His pulse ratcheted up as she rose to her toes and pressed a soft, lingering kiss against his cheek. Desire tore through him like a bullet, and he took a quick, deep breath.

McKenna's fingers tightened over his shoulders, but she didn't move away. Her lips brushed against his jawline.

He pressed his hand against the small of her back, tugging her closer. She moved fluidly toward him, her hips sliding against his, the friction delicious and hot. One slender hand curled around the back of his neck, tangling in his hair.

"You've let your hair grow," she murmured against his chin.

"I told you. I'm not the man you knew."

"Maybe that's a good thing." She lifted her gaze to meet his. "Maybe it's a good thing neither of us is the same person we were eight years ago."

"I'm not sure you're right about that," he murmured, his head dipping toward her. "But I find I don't care."

Her hand tightened on his neck, drawing him down to her. Her nose brushed against his as he slanted his head and closed the distance between them.

They had never done this, not once. There had been moments between them in Tablis when the sexual tension had been pure torture, moments when he'd wanted her with a ferocity that he'd never known with any other woman.

But they'd never closed the gap between them, never crossed that line.

Well, here he was. Here was the line, awaiting one more step.

His breath escaping his throat in a trembling sigh, he crossed it.

Chapter Seven

She'd wondered for a long time what it would be like to kiss Nick Darcy. Though she normally tried not to dwell on things that would never happen, she'd sometimes dreamed about kissing Darcy, imagined the feel of his mouth on hers during sleepless nights and even fantasized about what might happen next, whenever she wanted to distract herself from the stresses of her work.

Fantasies had seemed harmless enough, given the years and miles between her and the object of her unfulfilled desires. But mouth to mouth, body to body, drowning in the masculine scent of him, the heat of his hands sliding over the curve of her spine to settle low on her back, tugging her closer—he overwhelmed her utterly.

She felt hot all over. Hot and restless and rapidly losing control. He slid his hand beneath the hem of her T-shirt and up her back, his palms rough against her skin. Wrapping her arms around his neck, she pressed closer, flattening her body against his as he touched his tongue to hers, demanding a deeper response.

He pulled her closer, his arm tightening around her waist. His fingers dug into her side.

Her injured side.

Pain raced through her at his accidental touch, and she couldn't stop a sharp cry from escaping her lips.

He jerked back, releasing her, a stricken expression on his face. "Oh, God, I'm sorry."

"It's okay." Her voice came out a little breathless as she waited for the pain to ease.

"Let me take a look—I might have reopened your wounds."

"I think they're okay," she said as the pain settled down to a moderate ache.

"I am a complete idiot." His mortified tone tweaked her funny bone and she had to struggle against laughing.

"No, you're not." She caught his hand. "I'm fine."

"I should check to make sure it's not bleeding."

She arched her eyebrows. "Admit it, Darcy. You just want to get me naked."

He looked affronted. "Not at all!"

"Not even a little?" she asked with an exaggerated pout.

His expression softened. "You're having me on."

"I was trying to have you on. Me, that is. But then you freaked out like a virgin." She made a face at him. "Is that why you never put any moves on me all those years ago, Darcy? Performance anxiety?"

He smiled at that. "Now you're trying to bait me."

She took a step closer, knowing she was playing with fire. If she were a wise woman, she'd take advantage of this interruption and retreat to her corner. But not when Darcy looked so damned rumpled and sexy.

"Is it working?" she asked, her tone as sultry as she could manage.

"Am I tempted?" He dipped his head toward her, his breath warm and sweet against her cheek. "Absolutely."

"But?" she prodded, hearing the hesitation in his tone.

"But the last thing we need right now is a distraction. You're in danger, and we don't know from whom, exactly." He placed his hands on her shoulders, gently pushing her backward, putting distance between them. "Are you certain I don't need to check your wounds?"

"They're not even hurting anymore," she assured him, trying to quell her disappointment. He was right. She knew he was. The last thing either of them needed to do right now was drop their guard.

She was safe for the moment. Her wounds seemed to be healing, and so far, their efforts were keeping infection at bay. She was warm, dry, reasonably well rested and no longer completely alone.

It was time to stop running, she realized. Time to hunker down and come up with a plan other than "run as fast and far as you can."

"What are you thinking?" Darcy asked.

She looked up and found him watching her through narrowed eyes.

"You had a look on your face—" His lips quirked. "I've seen that look before. You've made a decision about something."

Her own lips curved in response. "I was just thinking that I've grown very weary of running."

"I'm sure you have."

"It's time to stop, don't you think?"

His eyebrows notched upward. "What do you have in mind?"

"I think," she said slowly, "it's time we sat down and devised a plan."

"A plan?"

She nodded. "I'm sick and tired of being the prey. I think it's time I became the hunter."

"CALVIN HOPKINS TOOK over after the Ridge County Sheriff's Department arrested Billy Dawson and his crew after they attempted the mass poisoning at the Highland Hotel and Resort." McKenna sat cross-legged on the sofa across from him, her fingers playing with the fringe of the sofa pillow she held in her lap.

Taking in the rise in her color and the return of strength and steadiness to her limbs, Darcy let himself begin to relax. They would have to remain aggressive with the fight against infection, but he was beginning to believe they might have caught it in time.

"Do I need to recap any of that part of the story?" she asked with a twitch of one eyebrow. "Or are you familiar with it?"

"I know about it," he assured her. He hadn't been directly on the Billy Dawson case, but everyone at The Gates knew how it had gone down. One of his fellow agents, Hunter Bragg, had infiltrated the Blue Ridge Infantry in time to uncover a plot to poison a convention full of federal, state and local law enforcement officers. Three hundred lives had been in danger before Hunter and the hotel's events planner, Susannah Marsh, had figured out the plot and found a way to foil it, despite the grave threat to their lives.

The same Susannah Marsh who'd turned out to be McKenna's cousin.

"Susannah told Quinn you and your mother helped her when she had to leave Boneyard Ridge to escape the Bradburys," he said.

She grimaced. "Sick bastards. One of those inbred monsters tried to rape a sixteen-year-old and she's the criminal because she shot him in self-defense?"

"She said she'd have never made it without you."

"She's family." McKenna shrugged.

It must be nice, he thought, to have family upon which to rely without question. In his own family, there had been love, of course, but also inflexible expectations. His father had been displeased by his choice to enter the security side of Foreign Service, dismissing his DSS position as nothing more than "a glorified security guard."

And his mother had been unhappy he'd chosen Foreign Service at all, hoping instead that he would stay near her in their Yorkshire country estate and help her raise and train racehorses.

"But you're good with the horses," she'd protested when he'd told her of his new career. "Do you realize how rare that really is? How many men and women in racing would kill for your natural talent with those beasts?"

He'd left England and his family behind, and most days, he had no regrets. Even now.

But sometimes—

"Hopkins had learned from Billy Dawson's mistakes. He was very careful who he let into the group. I knew I was never going to get into the inner circle as a woman. They're sexist pigs to the core."

"Then how did you propose to do it?"

"All I had to do was get inside once to set up the listening devices."

"And how did you accomplish that?"

"How does any woman infiltrate a group of men?" She smirked a little. "I showed them a little skin."

A cold, squirmy sensation jolted through him, settling in a queasy mass in the center of his stomach. "Which means?"

"One of them had a fortieth birthday coming up. So we started spreading flyers around Ridge County advertising private strip parties."

Another chill darted through him. "You stripped for them?" She let strange men—morally bankrupt reprobates— watch her undress?

Her lips curved in a smart-ass grin. "Oh, you thought I was the one who stripped? Hell, no. You know I'm the shy, retiring type. No, we hired a couple of girls from the go-go bar over in Barrowville, and they only stripped to their bikinis. I supervised the music, which included running wires and setting up the speakers—"

"And planting listening devices all about the room." Darcy started to relax.

"Yes. We knew the BRI had taken over the old lodge on Killshadow Road as their meeting place. We knew they'd held parties there before, even events like a community fundraiser for one of the BRI members who'd lost a leg in a car accident. We figured if we could get the place wired up, we might be able to find out exactly what they've got up their sleeve."

Darcy nodded. "But something went awry?"

"Not then. But a few days later, they had a couple of their anarchist hacker buddies in for a powwow and the hypervigilant nerd brought along a bug detector. They found the device and it didn't take long to narrow down the list of suspects to the maintenance crew they'd hired to clean up after the party or—"

"Or you," he finished for her.

"The maintenance crew was made up of family and friends. They shook them all down, scared the hell out of them and quickly figured out none of them was smart enough—or stupid enough—to pull off that kind of betrayal."

"Which left the strippers."

"And their DJ. The strippers were pretty well-known around town, and neither of them knew a thing about electronics, so it didn't take long to concentrate on me instead."

"Did you know your bug had been discovered?"

"The FBI did. I wasn't part of the listening crew. I was working other angles when it went down."

"Surely they warned you."

"They should have."

"But they didn't?"

She passed her hand slowly over her face. "There were

six people in the FBI who knew what I was doing, but only four count. The director himself and his deputy director signed off on everything, but they're not really in the day-to-day loop, so I'm not sure I should count them as suspects."

"Okay, who are the other four?"

"The Knoxville SAC, Glen Robertson, of course, and the SSA in charge of my unit, Darryl Boyle," she answered, glancing at him as if to gauge whether he knew what the acronyms meant.

He did, of course—working in a federal agency himself, he'd had contact with the FBI on numerous occasions. The SAC was the head of the field office where she'd worked, Knoxville in this case. The SSA was the Supervisory Special Agent directly in charge of her work as a special agent.

"Then there was Pete Chang, head of the Johnson City RA," she added, referring to the smaller resident agency located in a town northeast of Knoxville. "He assigned another special agent, Cade Landry, to work with me, since the BRI's territory in Tennessee straddles both jurisdictions."

He jotted the names down in the notebook app on his cell phone. "Okay, I can do a little digging around on these guys. Who was assigned to contact you about the discovery of your surveillance equipment?"

"SAC Robertson said he contacted both Agent Boyle and Agent Chang. Agent Boyle tried to reach me, but I was in a part of the mountains where cell reception was nil. Chang reached Landry, or so he said. Landry swears he didn't get any call from Chang about anything."

"Do you believe him?"

She frowned, clearly giving the question serious consideration. "I don't know," she said finally. "Landry—I think maybe he's a burnout. He does his job competently enough, but his heart's not in it."

Darcy knew the type. He'd gotten dangerously close to being one of those burnouts himself by the time he'd resigned from the DSS and taken Alexander Quinn up on the job offer with The Gates. "Apathetic, then? Or openly hostile toward being ordered around?"

"Not hostile," she said quickly. "If anything, he was too much the opposite. Nothing fazed him. Or interested him. He did his job because it was required of him, but there was no joy. No anger. No fire for justice. No fire at all."

"And you say he works out of the Johnson City RA?"

"Right. I think he was with the Richmond, Virginia, field office before that."

So, he'd moved from a bigger office to a resident agency, Darcy thought, jotting a note for himself. Sounded like a step down, not up, the bureau career ladder.

"Someone at The Gates was in the Johnson City RA before taking a job with us," he murmured. "I might be able to get her alone, away from the office, and pick her brain about Landry."

"You're talking about Ava Trent, right?"

"You know her?"

"I met her once or twice. Never worked with her. But yeah, I think she and Landry worked together on a couple of cases before she left the FBI."

"Before the BRI discovered the listening device, did you learn anything about their plans? You said the FBI believes they're plotting something very large and very deadly, yes?"

Her eyes narrowed at his tone. "You know something about that, don't you, Darcy?"

He gave himself a mental kick for not being more guarded with his thoughts and expressions. Despite eight years apart, he'd easily fallen back into the camaraderie he and McKenna had shared with the other "glorified security guards" watching over the US Embassy in Tablis. Despite the traditional interagency rivalries, people tasked with protecting America's diplomats in dangerous places had learned the hard way that working as a cohesive team was the only way to survive the challenges.

But was it a good idea to trust her with some of the secrets he and the other agents at The Gates had uncovered during their recent investigations into the criminal nexus between the Blue Ridge Infantry, an elusive group of black-hat anarchist hackers, and a loose confederation of methamphetamine manufacturers? A lot of good people had put their lives on the line for the information they'd helped gather. He wasn't going to betray their trust just to get on McKenna Rigsby's good side.

"You don't trust me?" She sounded both hurt and angry.

"I have to be careful. Some of the things I know are volatile."

"A lot of what I know is volatile. But I need your help, so I have to tell you what I know." She slanted a considering look at him. "Maybe then you'll tell me what you know and we'll both be better equipped to handle whatever kind of storm is blowing our way."

"Maybe." It was as much of a concession as he intended to offer until he heard more.

She blew out a breath, exasperation edging her expression. "Okay, fine. We think they're planning a domestic terror attack."

"Tell me something I don't know."

Her eyes narrowed. "So you do know more than you've said."

"I haven't said anything, so of course I do."

She narrowed her eyes further at him. "We don't think they'll try to repeat their plans from the attempted attack on the Tri-State Law Enforcement Society convention."

"No more poisoned béchamel?"

"Exactly. They're going for something bigger. I do know there's something up, something specific that they're planning. We were able to glean that much from their discussions before they discovered the bug."

"Just no details? No idea of the target?"

"Only that it will be big and very public."

"Of course," Darcy agreed. The point of any terrorist attack, domestic or foreign, was to incite fear and panic in the populace. "I suppose the more pertinent question is, what do they hope to accomplish? Do they have a goal beyond creating chaos?"

"That's the question, isn't it?" She unfolded her legs, stretching them out in front of her. She flexed her bare feet, pointing her toes, then curling them up toward her shin, as if stretching her calf muscles. For a moment, her concentration centered entirely on stretching and contracting her muscles, and Darcy found himself watching the bunching muscles of her calf with almost as much focus, imagining how those toned legs would feel beneath his touch.

When she spoke again, the sound of her voice sent a jolting ripple along his nerves. "There has to be something they hope to accomplish, but apparently nobody at the FBI can agree on what that could be." She looked up at him. "How about y'all? Anybody have a theory?"

"When our happy band of mismatched criminals was working for Wayne Cortland, figuring out what they wanted was easy enough," he said. "Cash."

"Which funded their individual projects, whatever those might be." She agreed with a brief nod. "That makes sense."

"But to stick together now, without that unifying entity, there has to be something else animating them. Something beyond cash."

"They all seem to hate the government."

"Many perfectly law-abiding people think ill of the government."

"But they don't conspire to poison a convention full of cops." She grimaced as she clasped her hands together and stretched her arms over her head. "There has to be something more specific than just some nebulous dislike for government."

"Unless they're planning to cripple the government in order to create the sort of chaotic conditions necessary for a revolt." Darcy knew firsthand how close the BRI had come to doing something just that massive only a month before.

"Cripple the government? You know as well as I do how many safeguards are in place to prevent governmental collapse."

"A month ago, the BRI was conspiring with hackers to shut down power to the eastern half of Tennessee, remember?"

"Creating trouble for half a small southern state is not the same as bringing down the federal government." She shook her head. "And that was really about Albert Morris and his greed, wasn't it? Morris was banking on the power failure to send state governments rushing to Cyber Solutions for help hardening their infrastructure against hacking—that's why he invested in so much of their stock."

"Morris was also trying to sell the federal government on Cyber Solutions," Darcy pointed out. "Which suggests he knew bigger attacks were on the horizon."

"But Morris was arrested and Cyber Solutions is under enormous scrutiny. What good would it do anyone to attempt another infrastructure attack?" McKenna shook her head, morning sunlight slanting through the cabin windows setting off sparks in the auburn curls dancing around her face. The urge to bury his face in those soft curls hit Darcy like a gut punch.

He dragged his gaze away, looking down at his clenched hands. "The only thing the BRI, their hacker mates and the drug dealers that help fund them have in common is a desire for chaos. So perhaps the more pertinent question is, what's driving the traitor in the FBI?"

McKenna's gaze snapped up to meet his. "That's a damned good question, isn't it?"

He nodded. "What benefit could someone in the FBI receive from letting a terrorist attack play out?"

Chapter Eight

"You told him about the GPS tracker?" Sunlight angling through the large window in Alexander Quinn's office set Olivia Sharp's face aglow and turned her eyes to a dazzling turquoise. Right now those turquoise eyes flashed angry fire at the occupant of the chair in front of Quinn's desk.

"I did." Cain Dennison sounded unapologetic. "I've also removed the one I found in my own truck," he added, looking away from Olivia and meeting Quinn's steady gaze. "And warned as many other agents as I've been able to talk to. If that's a problem for you, then I'll resign. But I'm not going to work for a company that treats me and the rest of the agents around here as if we're criminals who need to be tracked at all times."

"Fair enough," Quinn conceded. "I'll send out a memo to the other agents who'd like to have their trackers removed, as well."

"You're making my job twice as hard," Olivia protested.

"Work it out," Quinn said bluntly, his gaze leveling with hers until she looked away. He turned back to Dennison. "Have you informed Anson Daughtry, as well?"

Dennison nodded.

By the window, Olivia muttered a soft curse.

"I would have preferred that you had come to me first,"

Quinn told Dennison, "but I do understand your sense of violation."

"Why did you do it, then?"

Quinn folded his hands in front of him, not sure how to answer. Old habits died hard, true, but he should have known better than to play games with his agents' lives. One of the reasons he'd left the CIA after so many years with the agency had been his increasing disgust with the way the government viewed its agents as pawns in a high-risk game. It had ever been so, of course, and probably would be so for as long as a dangerous world required spy games to keep the planet from going up in flames.

But people used to matter. They had value beyond their usefulness. The spy game had never been fair or above-board, but the players used to be more than just human chess pieces.

He'd almost forgotten that himself, more than once. Had let the game control him when he should have been controlling the game.

People had died. People who shouldn't have.

"I forgot who I am," he said finally, meeting Dennison's gaze without flinching. "I forgot why I'm here."

Dennison's eyes narrowed but he gave a short nod. "We all do, sometimes."

"You're right." Olivia walked away from the window and dropped with casual grace into the seat next to Dennison, crossing one long leg over the other. "One of the reasons I left the FBI was to get away from this sort of game-playing. I'm sorry."

"Look, I know we all want to find out who among us is leaking information. But if we're all going around suspicious of everybody, it's going to kill our ability to work as a team." Dennison stood up. "For the record, I don't think for a second Nick Darcy is the mole. He doesn't have a treacherous bone in his body."

"We have to do the investigation," Olivia said. "We can't assume anything."

"I know that. But I don't think he's going to listen to anything else I have to say." Dennison pulled a well-worn baseball cap from the back pocket of his jeans and pulled it over his head. He tipped the brim toward Olivia, then shot a long, hard look at Quinn. "If you want someone spying on him, you'll need to find another agent."

Olivia's gaze followed Dennison from the room. "Perhaps I made a bad choice with that one."

"You were looking for an agent Darcy considers a friend," Quinn said. "Dennison is as close as it gets."

"Darcy's quite a loner."

Quinn shot her a pointed look.

Her lips curved slightly. "Touché. But I have good reasons for my curmudgeonly ways."

"As does Darcy." Quinn leaned back in his chair, steepling his fingers over his stomach. "For the moment, he and Agent Rigsby are safe. He'll protect her because he knows I want him to. And because he has a connection to her."

"A connection?"

"An old one. But he's the one she went to when she was in trouble." Quinn had seen signs that the pretty FBI agent and the quiet, serious DSS agent were forming a special connection, though he'd never detected any sign that they'd crossed a line. Wouldn't have been his business if they had, though knowing all the secrets inside the embassy had been part of his job as a CIA operative.

"What do we know about her problems with the bureau?" Olivia asked, curiosity sparking behind her bright eyes.

"The only word we're getting is that she's gone rogue. She disobeyed an order from her superiors and is now considered a compromised asset."

"And we have no idea what that order might have been?"

Quinn sat up straight. "She was asked to meet a fellow agent for extraction from an undercover assignment."

"Undercover doing what?"

"That's the question."

Olivia was silent for a moment, her gaze lowered to her folded hands. When she looked up again, Quinn didn't miss the worry in her eyes. "There's something you're not telling me, isn't there? Is it about Landry?"

He'd wondered when she would get around to asking that question. "Landry was assigned to the same investigation Agent Rigsby was on."

"But he's out of Johnson City. You said Rigsby was working out of the Knoxville Field Office."

"Joint operation."

Olivia's fingers threaded together, her grip so tight that her knuckles began to whiten. "Has he gone rogue, as well?"

"Not to my knowledge."

She relaxed visibly. "Do you want me to try to find another agent to replace Dennison on the Nick Darcy investigation?"

Quinn shook his head. "Dennison was the best you were going to get. I'll cover it myself. I think he still trusts me enough to stay in touch if he needs help."

"You don't think he's responsible for the leaks, do you?"

"I don't." Quinn looked up at her. "I don't think Daughtry is responsible, either. But they were the only other agents who knew about Mallory Jennings and her work here. Someone leaked that information to some very bad people. So we have to look closely at both Darcy and Daughtry."

"If you don't think it's one of them—"

"I don't think either of them would leak the information intentionally."

"But you don't know whether it might have been an accident," Olivia finished the thought for him. "So maybe I should be looking at the people around them?"

Quinn opened his desk drawer and pulled out a folder. "I've surveyed three months of security video and compiled every contact between Darcy, Daughtry and other agents and support staff. The notes are here." He handed the folder to Olivia. "Have fun."

She took the folder, her eyes narrowing. "You want me to do background checks on all the people those two have come into contact with for the past three months?"

"Yes."

She released her breath on a long, slow sigh. "Can I have some agents to help me out?"

"Sure." Quinn waved his hand at the folder. "Anybody who's not working another case and isn't on that list of contacts."

She shot him a hard look. "You've got to be kidding me. Everybody in the office is probably on this list."

"I culled the list to support staff. If none of those pan out, then we'll start looking at field agents."

"Fine." She slapped the folder against her hip and stalked out of the office, looking like a pissed-off swan as she floated out the door, slamming it behind her.

Quinn couldn't hold back a smile.

"I DON'T THINK it can be either the FBI director or his deputy, so we can mark them off the list." Darcy came back from the kitchen with a bowl of soup for each of them. He set the bowls on the coffee table between them and pulled spoons wrapped in paper towels from the pocket of his jeans. "Here you go."

McKenna took the spoon and dipped it into the thick broth. "What is this?"

"Hearty beef and vegetable, or so the can said." He pulled the armchair closer to the footlocker doubling as a coffee table. "It's fluids and nutrition, both of which you need, so eat up."

The soup was pretty good for something out of a can, and she was hungrier than she'd thought. She'd consumed almost half the bowl before she realized Darcy was watching her.

"What?" she asked, wiping her mouth with a napkin.

He smiled. "Glad to see your appetite is coming back. You used to eat like a horse when we were working at the embassy."

"Yeah, well, that was eight years ago. Oh, to be young again."

"You still look great."

A flutter of pure feminine pleasure darted through her. "Back at ya."

"There are more cans in the kitchen if that's not enough."

"This should be plenty." She put her spoon down for a minute, not wanting to eat so quickly she made herself sick. She hadn't had a decent meal in a couple of days, so she'd have to ease her stomach into being full again. "I don't think my SAC would betray me," she said, playing with the corner of her napkin. "So that leaves my supervisory special agent, Darryl Boyle, the head of the Johnson City RA, Pete Chang—"

"And Cade Landry."

Something about Darcy's tone made her sit up straighter. "Do you know something about Landry I should know?"

He shook his head. "Just that he worked a case recently that The Gates ended up getting involved in."

"Was it Susie's case?" She didn't remember her cousin mentioning any involvement with the FBI, but there was a lot about her life that Susie—Susannah—hadn't told McKenna.

"No. It was earlier than that. He was assigned to a case involving a married couple ambushed and abducted from their motel room—"

"Oh, right. That's the case where it came out that Sinclair Solano was still alive. And not really a traitor." Some of the people she worked with hadn't been happy about learning they'd spent years and resources hunting a fugitive that the CIA knew was one of the good guys. "Let me guess—Quinn was the CIA agent who failed to inform all the other pertinent government agencies that Solano wasn't actually a terrorist."

"Not only that, but Solano is working for Quinn now. And recently married Ava Trent."

"Wow. Didn't see that coming."

"They both joined The Gates around the same time, and though they tried to be circumspect about it, it's difficult to hide when one is madly in love." Darcy's smile was close to a grimace. "Confirmed singles are dropping like flies around that office these days. I'm beginning to wonder if Quinn has slipped something into the water."

"You're such a romantic, Darcy."

His smile faded. "Romance is folly. Better to join oneself to another, if that's what you choose, with your eyes open and your heart intact."

"Is that what your parents did?"

He made a face. "God, no. Well, my father did, I suppose. He weighed my mother's qualities and assets and found her an appropriate mate for a man in his position."

"But your mother fell in love?"

"She did. Just not with my father."

"Oh."

"Nothing came of it. Nothing ever could have. He was married and a peer. She was married to an American diplomat." Darcy pushed his half-empty soup bowl away. "Love is a mercurial bitch."

"So that's why—" She stopped, not sure she cared to hear the answer to her unspoken question. "Never mind. So you think Ava Trent could help us find out more about Cade Landry?"

"Maybe. Probably could give us a pretty good bead on whether Pete Chang is the sort of man who'd leak information to the BRI, as well."

A flicker of excitement burbled in her chest at the thought she might be one step closer to finding out who had put a target on her back. "Do you think you could risk giving her a call and picking her brain?"

"I'd prefer to meet face-to-face," Darcy answered. "She may suspect more about one or the other of them than she's willing to share on the phone. I can press her for more information if I see she's holding something back."

"Can I go with you?"

He slanted a quelling look at her. "No."

"She doesn't have to know who I am."

"I'm fairly sure Quinn will have passed along the FBI all-points bulletin. It's standard procedure at the agency when such information comes our way. If he didn't, and someone discovered the omission, it would raise questions about why he failed to do so."

"Questions Quinn wouldn't want to answer."

"Exactly." He nodded at her mostly empty bowl as he picked up his own and rose to his feet. "Are you done?"

She pushed the bowl toward him. "Yes, thanks."

When he returned from the kitchen, he picked up the leather jacket he'd left draped over his chair. "I'll drop by the office and see if I can track down Ava. You should lie down and get some rest."

"I'm not tired," she protested.

"Doesn't matter. Your body needs rest if you're serious about speeding up your recuperation time." He arched a dark eyebrow at her. "You are serious about getting better soon, aren't you?"

She controlled the urge to hurl one of the throw pillows from the sofa at him. "Of course I am."

"Find a book to read." He waved his hand at the built-in

bookshelves that flanked the hearth. "Or find a radio and listen to some music, if you can find a station around here that plays anything other than hillbilly anthems. Oh, wait, you are a hillbilly—"

"Not a hillbilly, Jeeves."

Shrugging on the jacket, he shot her a grin. "Not a Brit, Elly May."

She managed to hold back her smile until he was safely out the door.

THE VISITOR'S BADGE clipped to the waistband of his jeans flapped as he walked down the corridor to the agents' bull pen, a nagging reminder that he was no longer one of them. Not in any meaningful way.

There were only a handful of agents in the office at this time of day. Fortunately for Darcy, Ava Trent—Solano, he amended mentally—was one of them.

She looked up at him, her hazel eyes brightening. "Darcy!"

"Hey, Ava." He pulled a nearby metal-and-vinyl chair up to her desk and sat. "Where's Sin?"

"Out on a case." She lowered her voice. "Quinn still won't let us share a case. I think we'll probably be celebrating our twentieth anniversary before he trusts us not to get distracted by each other."

"I've seen the two of you," Darcy said with a smile. "Quinn's probably right, you know."

She laughed. "Probably. What brings you here? Quinn's reinstating you, I hope?"

"Not yet," he said with a sigh. "Actually, I'm looking into something that's sort of fallen into my lap. A personal issue, I guess you could say, regarding someone I worked with several years ago."

Ava twisted her wavy brown hair into a knot and stuck a pencil through the twist to hold the makeshift chignon in place before she bent closer. "A personal issue? Do tell."

"Could we take a walk?"

She shot him a puzzled look but stood and grabbed her jacket from the back of her chair. "If Quinn asks, tell him I'm taking my break," she told the nearest agent, a tall blonde who had come on board a couple of days before Quinn had put him on administrative leave. Olivia Sharp—he finally placed her as she turned to give Ava a quizzical look.

"We get breaks?" she drawled.

Ava just grinned and looked at Darcy. "So, you have a personal problem? You need a woman's viewpoint? Advice?"

What was it with people in love? They couldn't seem to bear it if the rest of the world didn't find a way to pair up, two by two.

"It's not that sort of personal issue," he said, quickly shoving the memory of kissing McKenna Rigsby to the back of his mind. "It's a former colleague who's run into some trouble with the FBI."

Ava looked faintly puzzled. "And because I used to work for the FBI you thought—"

"Actually, you used to work with the Johnson City resident agency, and that's why I'm here. What can you tell me about a special agent named Cade Landry?"

A loud thud behind him made him jump. He turned in time to see Olivia Sharp crouching to gather up a stack of files she'd dropped.

"I didn't work with Landry for long," Ava said, drawing his gaze back to her. "Really only a month or two before I left the bureau to come work here. Why do you want to know something about Landry?"

He took the jacket from her hands and helped her into it. "Let's walk," he said.

Ava led Darcy out of the bull pen and down the hall, where he relinquished his visitor's badge to the receptionist.

Outside, the sun was dipping toward the west, taking with it most of the day's heat. Ava kept pace with Darcy's longer legs as they headed east on Magnolia Drive.

"What do you want to know about Landry?"

"Have you seen the APB from the FBI regarding a rogue agent?"

Ava's eyes narrowed. "I have. You think Landry might be involved with this missing agent?"

"Something like that."

Her lips tightened to a tight line. "I don't like to speak ill of people when they're not here to defend themselves."

"But you know something?"

She lowered her voice. "If you're asking me if I have any proof that Cade Landry is a crooked agent, no. I don't."

"So what *do* you know?"

"I know that he has an impressive job jacket. Great scores at the Academy, commendations out the wazoo from his first weeks and months on the job. He was going somewhere. Fast. And then—"

"And then?" he prodded when she fell silent.

She released a deep sigh. "About a year ago, he started going downhill quickly. Went from a blue-flamer heading up the ladder in the Richmond Field Office to a glorified grunt in the Johnson City RA. He was actually junior to me, even though he had more years of experience. That doesn't happen unless something has gone very, very wrong."

"But you have no idea what?"

She shook her head. "I didn't stick around that long, and it wasn't like I was looking to become his confessor."

"What was he like to work with?"

Ava's brow creased. "Apathetic. He went through the motions, did the work adequately enough, but I could tell he really didn't have any heart for the job. I know there are some agents who try to maintain a certain distance from the work—it's probably smart, since I've seen a lot of agents get too close to their cases and end up in long-term therapy before it was all over—but with Landry, it wasn't even about keeping his professional distance. He really didn't seem to care about anything at all."

"Any theories as to why?"

"Like I said, I didn't ask any questions and he didn't offer any answers. I'm pretty sure that whatever went wrong went wrong when he was in Richmond, though. Because before Richmond, he was fast-tracking it to the top. And then his forward progress just seemed to stop."

"Do you know if it could have been related to his personal life? A broken marriage? Death of a loved one?"

"He was never married. That much I got out of him on a stakeout once." Ava shook her head. "As for a family member dying? I don't know. He didn't mention any family at all while we worked together in Johnson City. I wish I could tell you more."

"That's helpful, truly." He could do some digging into Landry's public records, see if he could find something about the man's family. An emotional upheaval could lead an otherwise stable man off the deep end, and deep ends were exactly where a crew of parasites like the BRI and their criminal comrades could do a lot of damage.

"Is that all you needed?"

"Just one more question. What can you tell me about Pete Chang?"

Ava's expression darkened. "He's a jerk. A total brown-noser trying to move his way up to a better assignment. He's an FBI man through and through."

"Could he be compromised? Could he be corrupted?"

"Chang? Not by anyone outside the FBI, no." Her lips flattened. "Now, if someone in the FBI gave him a shady order, and he thought it could give him a boost up the bureau ladder? He'd be tempted. But I don't know that I think he'd even do something corrupt then. He'd probably think it was a test or a trap and report the overture up the chain of command."

"Ah, one of those."

Her lips quirked. "I imagine you had dealings with that type of bureaucrat working at State."

"I did indeed." He managed a smile, hoping it didn't appear too much like a grimace. "Thank you for the information."

"Anytime." She started to turn toward the old Victorian mansion Quinn had turned into The Gates, then stopped and looked back at Darcy. "This is about that FBI agent on the run, isn't it?"

He didn't answer. He could see in her eyes he didn't have to.

"Do you trust her?"

He didn't answer that question, either, but whatever Ava saw in his expression seemed to satisfy her.

"Be careful." Her smile held considerable concern.

"Always am." He watched her walk back down the sidewalk to The Gates, wishing he could go with her, not as a visitor but back at his desk, working the job he hadn't realized he'd come to enjoy so much until he'd been barred from doing it.

He tried not to speed on his way back to the cabin, but he didn't like leaving McKenna alone so long. She was making a good show of being stronger, but he'd seen the circles of fatigue under her eyes, the pale tone of her skin. She was still weak, still vulnerable.

And he felt a driving need to protect her.

About three miles from the turnoff, a glance in the rearview mirror made him sit up straighter. That black SUV about three cars back had been with him since he'd left The Gates, hadn't it?

He took the next turnoff and drove at a steady pace down one of the small feeder roads that led toward Warrior Creek

Falls. Only one vehicle behind him followed, keeping a steady distance from him. The black SUV.

He was being tailed.

Chapter Nine

She'd tried to nap, but the cabin was entirely too quiet. At her place in Knoxville, there was a constant flow of background noise that never let her feel alone—traffic on the street outside her window, the hum of electrical appliances not only in her place but in those nearby, the whisper of heated air coming through the vents to warm the drafty old four-room apartment.

Here in the middle of nowhere, surrounded by nothing but trees and nervous little woodland creatures, the silence was nearly complete. The hiss of the space heater set into the hearth was the only noise, and though it was quiet, in the dearth of ambient noise, it seemed to ring through her head like whispered conversations just out of earshot. The effect was creepy and not at all conducive to sleep.

So when the phone rang just as she started to finally doze off, it set off dozens of little explosions along her nervous system, jerking her wide awake in a second.

The digital readout on the phone's display showed a number but no name. What was Darcy's number? She tried to calm her shattered nerves enough to remember.

Taking a chance, she picked up the phone but didn't speak.

"Rigsby?" Darcy's clipped accent rang over the line.

She slumped against the sofa cushions. "Yes."

"Listen carefully. I've picked up a tail. I'm trying to shake it, but you need to be prepared in case someone already suspects where we're staying. I'm fairly sure Bragg has extra firearms stashed somewhere in the cabin. You know he's worried about those hillbilly hotheads from over in Boneyard Ridge coming after Susannah."

McKenna knew well the potential threat to her cousin's life. She and her mother had taken Susie in when she was just sixteen, hiding her from a family of meth-dealing criminals determined to make her pay for killing one of their own when he tried to rape her. The Bradburys hadn't stopped looking for a chance to serve a little mountain justice to McKenna's cousin, finally catching up to her a few months ago.

If it weren't for Hunter Bragg and his colleagues at The Gates, Susie would probably be dead now. The agents from The Gates had issued a stern warning to the Bradburys that Susie was under their protection now. So far, the truce had held, but McKenna knew Hunter and Susie would always feel the need to keep their guard up.

"I'll look around," she said. "I'm armed, as well." Her Glock's magazine could hold thirteen rounds, but she'd used some rounds in getting away from the people who'd shot her. She had only nine rounds left. She needed to go ammo shopping soon.

"Listen closely. If you get surrounded, there's a way out of the cabin you need to know about." Darcy's voice was low and tight over the phone. "Downstairs in the basement, there's a big armoire near the back. Open the door and step inside. There's a pressure plate in the floor of the armoire that opens a trapdoor."

"How do you know about that?"

"Quinn told me."

"How does Quinn know?" As soon as she asked the question, she felt like an idiot. "Never mind. How does Quinn know anything? He's magic."

Darcy's soft chuckle bolstered her spirits. "If I can shake the tail, I'll be back. If I can't—if you don't hear something from me within an hour—I want you to take that basement escape tunnel. It comes out several yards into the woods. You'll need to start hiking due north. Within half a mile, you'll see a big mountain over the top of the trees. That's Laurel Rise. Keep hiking. You'll come upon a gravel road eventually. Follow that road up the mountain until you reach a big cabin at the top. That cabin belongs to Quinn. I've already called to tell him he might be getting a visitor."

Her gut tightened painfully. She wasn't sure what scared her more—the thought of hiking up a mountain in her weakened condition or coming face-to-face with Alexander Quinn again after all these years.

"Can you do that, Rigsby?" Darcy asked when she didn't respond.

She squared her shoulders. "Yes."

"I will do my best to get back to you." His voice held a hint of steel.

"I know."

He hung up without saying goodbye.

For a moment, she sat very still, still gripping the phone in one hand as her mind reeled beneath an onslaught of mental orders—find another weapon, find ammo, pack tools and necessities, pack water and food.

She shook off the paralysis and pushed to her feet, ignoring the punch of pain in her side. She didn't have time to indulge her weakness.

Her life was in danger, and once again, she had to figure out a way to save herself.

DARCY WAS RUNNING out of time, but he had to be sure he'd lost the tail—and any possible backup tail—before he risked going back to McKenna. She was depending on him to keep her safe, and the last thing he wanted to do was fail her the way—

He stopped himself short. He had to stop beating himself up over the past. The embassy siege had been eight years ago. He'd been concussed and outnumbered, along with those DSS and Marine Security Guard troops who'd survived the initial onslaught. Despite the wishful thinking of State Department bureaucrats sitting in their fancy offices in Washington, DC, there had been no way to get through that sort of relentless, vicious terrorist attack without sustaining casualties.

The real surprise had been just how many people had survived the siege, thanks to the efforts of people like Maddox Heller, McKenna Rigsby and, yes, even him.

He just didn't like losing. And so many dead embassy employees was a loss. No way around it.

He hadn't seen the black SUV in fifteen minutes. He'd backtracked, raced through yellow traffic lights, taken quick turns without signaling and broken about a dozen traffic laws trying to shake his followers, but there was still a vehicle behind him, about a hundred yards back. He couldn't make out much about it, except it was a lighter color. He couldn't even be sure if it was the same vehicle he'd spotted earlier, before he lost the black SUV.

Just in case, he whipped left down a side road that led toward Deception Lake and parked near a lakeside cabin. The place looked closed up for the season; April in the Smokies was still cool enough to dissuade tourists and part-time mountain dwellers from opening up their cabins until the advent of summer.

He got out of the Land Rover and hiked deeper into the woods, settling behind a large mountain laurel bush that offered both cover and a decent vantage point to watch the road.

After ten minutes with no sign of a following vehicle,

he returned to the Land Rover and settled behind the steering wheel, letting his racing pulse return to normal before he pulled his phone from his pocket and called Bragg's cabin again.

McKenna answered on the first ring, her voice tight. "Where are you?"

"On the road," he answered. "Listen to me. I still don't think it's safe for me to come straight back to the cabin, but if you haven't seen any sign of intruders, you're probably safe enough for now. Try not to worry. I'll be back there as soon as I can."

"Where are you going?"

He started the Land Rover, his muscles bunching with tension as the engine roared to life. "I think it's time I go talk to an old friend and find out just what the hell he's up to."

"I'M NOT HAVING you followed." Quinn kept his tone calm, though the man pacing the floor in front of his desk was anything but placid.

Nick Darcy halted suddenly, bending forward and slapping his hands on Quinn's desk. Though a lean man, he was tall and broad-shouldered, big enough to be imposing when he wanted to. If Quinn had been a different sort of man, he might have felt intimidated.

Instead, he mostly felt annoyed. And curious.

"You had a GPS tracker attached to my vehicle."

"I had them attached to every agent's vehicle."

"Without our consent?"

"Technically, I do have your consent," Quinn answered calmly. "Perhaps you should have read the fine print on your contract more closely."

Darcy's nostrils flared. "I'm on administrative leave."

"Doesn't negate your contract."

"Perhaps not. But I removed the tracker. And I'll be

checking my vehicle every time I leave here in order to be certain you haven't attached another. Is that clear?"

Quinn ignored the question. "Why do you think I'm having you followed?"

"Because it's the sort of thing you'd do," Darcy snapped.

Quinn quelled an unexpected flicker of dismay. He hadn't started The Gates to be anyone's friend. Everyone he'd hired had been brought into the company because hc believed they could be valuable assets, not because he liked them personally or cared to be thought of as a friend.

He wasn't Darcy's friend. He wasn't anyone's friend.

But he valued Darcy's opinion, nevertheless. He supposed their long and often-colorful history together had made Darcy the closest thing Quinn had to a friend. He knew Darcy's thoughts on most subjects because the former DSS agent had been relentlessly honest with him, for good or for bad.

He didn't like hearing the disgust in Darcy's voice.

"I'm not having you followed," he said bluntly. "If I were, you would never have spotted the tail."

Darcy's lips flattened to a thin line.

"I am curious, however," Quinn continued, "why you spirited one of my agents out of here this afternoon for a private chat."

"Did she tell you?"

Quinn shook his head. "No."

"But you know about it."

"Of course."

Darcy sighed, dropping heavily into one of the chairs in front of Quinn's desk. "Do you know what we were talking about?"

"No. Would you like to tell me?"

Darcy was silent for a long moment, his dark eyes studying Quinn with disquieting intensity. Whatever he saw in Quinn's face seemed to answer some unspoken question, for his tense shoulders relaxed, and he nodded. "I wanted some information on an FBI agent named Cade Landry. Ava used to work with him at the FBI's Johnson City RA."

Quinn kept his expression carefully blank. "What did you want to know about him?"

"What kind of agent he was. Whether he could be turned."

"Did Trent have an opinion on the subject?"

"She shared her impressions of Agent Landry. We didn't come to a concrete conclusion."

"You know if you want my help, you need only ask."

"If I want your help, I will ask."

Quinn wasn't going to hold his breath. "If you care to know, the internal investigation into your activities over the past few months has nearly concluded. We should have something to share with you in a week or two."

"Kind of you." There was no warmth in Darcy's tone as he rose to his feet and started toward the door.

"I'm not your enemy," Quinn said, though he'd had no intention of speaking.

Darcy turned in the doorway to look at him. "But you're not my friend, either. Are you?"

Quinn had no answer to offer.

Darcy turned and left Quinn's office, letting the door click shut behind him.

Quinn sat in silence for a long moment, trying to clear his head. It wasn't like him to be thrown by the doubts of one of his agents. He knew most of them weren't certain they could trust his motives. They were probably right. He'd been working angles for so long, he wasn't sure he knew how to stop.

But he wasn't dealing Darcy an unfair hand, no matter what the agent thought. He was playing it straight as a board, giving Darcy all the leeway he could spare out of respect for their shared history.

Sooner or later, he hoped, Darcy would see what the

truth really was. And while he might never earn his cautious agent's friendship, he hoped he might earn back a measure of respect.

Three sharp raps on his door drew him out of his speculations. Before he could speak, the door opened and Olivia Sharp entered. "Was that Nick Darcy I just saw leaving?"

Quinn sighed. "You may enter."

Olivia made a face and dropped with easy grace into the chair Darcy had just vacated. "What did he want?"

Quinn was tempted to tell her to mind her own business, but he was becoming very curious about Olivia's connection to Cade Landry. "He spoke with Ava Trent about someone she used to work with."

Olivia's blue eyes went diamond hard, but that was the only change in her carefully schooled expression. "Why?"

"He wanted to know if Ava thought the man might be corrupt."

Olivia didn't blink. Her facial expression never changed. But most of the color leached from her cheeks, and her eyes went positively glacial. "It's Cade Landry. Isn't it?"

Well, Quinn thought, *isn't that interesting?*

TRY TO RELAX.

McKenna almost laughed aloud at the thought. Darcy hadn't shown up yet, though he'd called to reassure her she was probably safe. She'd been sitting there in the cabin's small front room, fondling her Glock and watching the minute hand on her watch go around the dial.

She wasn't sure she'd ever relax again.

The sound of footfalls on the porch steps sent a rattle through her nerves. She picked up the Glock from the coffee table and rose, willing herself to remain calm and focused.

The steps outside seemed to belong to only one pair of feet. She had nine rounds in the Glock. She liked her odds.

The door rattled and started to open. She settled in a shooter's stance and lifted the Glock.

The door stopped moving. Darcy's voice came cautiously through the narrow opening. "Rigsby? Are you aiming your weapon at the door?"

"I am."

"Please don't."

Unable to quell a nervous smile, she lowered the Glock, though she kept it gripped in one hand, ready to aim again if Darcy wasn't alone.

But he was. And he was bearing two large canvas bags that looked full of—

"Groceries," he announced, kicking the door shut behind him.

"You amazing man." She followed him to the kitchen and pulled up a chair while he started putting food away.

"I detect a hint of cupboard love in that declaration," he said with a smile, waggling a chocolate bar in front of her. "Your sweet tooth still in working condition?"

She grabbed the bar and set it on the table beside her. "It is, thank you. What else did you get?"

"I went for packaged frozen meals and canned foods. I know fresh would be better, but we may not have time to cook, and we might as well put the microwave to good use."

"Good point." She looked through the selection of meals he'd chosen, spotting several of her favorites. She and Darcy had shared lunch together dozens of times while working closely in Tablis; had he remembered her food preferences after all this time?

"However, since I was in town and the place was right there, I did stop and get this for our dinner." He pulled a large paper bag from one of the canvas totes and set it on the table between them. "There's a place in Purgatory called Tabbouleh Garden that serves the best falafel wraps I've had since I left the Middle East."

She opened the sack, breathing in the spicy aromas. In an instant, she was starving. "Definitely the most amazing man in the world. Though my hips may not thank you for the extra pounds they're about to pack on."

While she crossed to the sink to wash her hands, he put away the last of the groceries, finishing by the time she dried her hands and returned to the table. He turned to gaze at her, leaning back against the counter and crossing his arms as he gave her a look warm enough to make her spine tingle. "Rigsby, here's something you may not know. Most men—myself included—enjoy curves on women. And as delicious as yours clearly are, you're in no danger of 'packing on' too much flesh anytime soon. So indulge yourself." He smiled. "I used to enjoy watching you eat."

She didn't know whether to feel flattered or self-conscious. She settled on a little of both. "So *that's* what you were doing. I just thought you were grading my table manners on a scale from redneck to royalty."

He smiled at her lame joke as he turned to wash his hands at the sink. "Middle Eastern food is meant to be eaten with the hands. With gusto and appreciation for the flavors and textures." He dried his hands, pulled up a chair and reached into the bag, coming back with a container of hummus. He removed the top and set it on the table in front of them.

"You're right," she agreed. She looked in the bag and found something wrapped in aluminum foil. She set the packet on the table in front of them and peeled off the foil. "Mmm, pitas."

He took one of the pita rounds, tore it in half and handed another piece to her. He took his half, folded it into a scoop shape and dug right into the hummus. "So, how are my table manners now?"

"As much as I want to say closer to redneck than royalty, you somehow manage to look regal no matter what you're doing." She copied his actions, dipping hummus onto her half of the pita. A dollop of the spicy chickpea puree started to fall from the makeshift scoop. She caught it with her mouth, but not before some of it plopped onto her chin.

As she reached to wipe it away, he caught her hand, his dark eyes glittering with a dangerously sexy light. "Allow me," he murmured, releasing her hand and reaching up to slide his forefinger across her chin, catching the drop of hummus on the tip. He offered the tip of his finger to her. "Don't want to miss a drop."

Heat flooded her core and spread like wildfire along her nerve endings. Her heart pounding, she caught his hand in hers and drew his fingertip to her lips. Tentatively, she licked the creamy dip from his finger, then sucked lightly to catch every bit.

Darcy's eyes darkened as she finally released his hand.

"What are we doing?" Her voice came out hoarse and strangled.

Darcy rose slowly from his chair, sending it scraping back across the tile floor. McKenna found herself on her feet, as well, without quite remembering how she got there. As Darcy moved around the table toward her, she felt the tidal pull of him, drawing her relentlessly closer, steel to his magnet.

"I don't know," he answered her question as his head bent toward hers.

Then he kissed her, and she was lost.

Chapter Ten

Maybe it was the residual adrenaline coursing through his body. Or his growing sense of frustration at being relegated to what bloody well felt like house arrest. Or, if he was being perfectly honest, it might be his rather lengthy recent drought when it came to female company in his bed.

Whatever the cause, deep down he knew, even as he swept McKenna more tightly into his embrace, that kissing her was the absolute wrong thing to do.

Except it felt right. So right. She fit against him so perfectly, smelled so enticing, kissed him back with such a heady combination of honey and fire that he wanted to surround himself with her, breathe her into his lungs, taste the sweet heat of her mouth on his until she consumed him.

Was this how it would have been eight years ago if they'd given in to the temptation that had tormented them both? Or was the reward that much greater for having denied themselves so long?

Her tongue slid against his, tasting, testing, and he drank deeply from the well of her passion.

When she withdrew from him, tugging free of his embrace, the sudden loss of her soft heat felt like a jolting shock to his system.

"We can't do this, Darcy."

"Clearly, we can," he disagreed, reaching for her again.

She dodged his grasp, crossing the kitchen until her back was pressed against the refrigerator door. "Listen to me. We can't do this. Too much is at stake to be taking chances like this. This is why we stayed away from each other all those years ago. You know it is. It's just the business we're in."

Frustration burned in his gut. "People in this business have sex all the time. They take lovers. They take wives and husbands. They have flings, one-night stands, lifelong passions. They don't stop living. Why should we?"

"Which is it, Darcy?" She took a step toward him, her hands on her hips. Her unruly curls undulated around her head like Medusa's snakes, making him wonder if she was about to strike him dead with her crystalline gaze. "Is this going to be meaningless sex? Friends with benefits? Is it supposed to be a real relationship? What's it going to be?"

He stared back at her, at a loss for an answer. What *was* he expecting from her? Did he even know?

"That's what I thought." She pushed her hands through her hair and the auburn coils calmed beneath her touch, making him wonder what those magic hands could do to his body. Would he, too, grow gentle and compliant under her caress, or would she set him ablaze with every stroke?

He wanted it all. The tranquillity and the chaos. But he saw from the wary, rigid set of her posture that telling the truth would only drive her further away.

He couldn't risk it.

"So you're saying we can't touch each other?"

"I'm not sure we could avoid that, living in the same small cabin," she murmured, looking away as if the directness of his gaze was more than she could bear. "We just need to be professionals."

"Not friends?"

Her gaze snapped up to meet his. "We're friends. That's the one thing I'm sure about. You—" Her voice broke suddenly, and to his surprise, tears welled in her eyes. She cleared her throat and started again. "You got me through one of the scariest, most traumatic experiences of my life. And the fact that I didn't trust myself to stay in touch with you doesn't mean I didn't miss you in my life every single day."

Her words were so stark, so brave, so true to his own experience that he felt tears prick his own eyes. He blinked them away before they could fully form. "I didn't know."

"Of course you didn't." A smile curved her lips, and she knuckled away her own tears. "I worked damned hard not to let you know."

"I missed you, too," he admitted with a smile of his own. "Part of me wonders if I didn't take the job with The Gates so I could be surrounded by hillbilly accents like yours."

"Not a hillbilly." Still smiling, she rolled her eyes and returned to the table, opening the sack from the restaurant to dig inside. Her gaze rose to meet his as he took his own seat. "Oh, Darcy. You bought baklava, you wicked, wonderful man."

Pleasure flooded through him on a wave of warmth. "You loved that baklava you used to buy at that little sweetshop near the embassy. You even shared once in a while."

"Well, don't get your hopes up this time, hotshot. I'm starving." She tugged the sticky layered squares closer, flashing him a bright grin.

Too bright, he thought. She was trying to behave as if everything was fine. But she knew as well as he did that nothing was fine. She was in trouble. He had barely shaken a tail that afternoon. They had suspects but no proof that she'd been set up by people in her own bureau.

And they'd come damned close to going straight from tentative friends to reckless lovers in the span of a few minutes.

She was pure temptation. He had tried to pretend otherwise, tried to blame his lack of self-control around her on his recent romantic drought or the volatile emotions she'd unearthed by her mere presence, a part of his past with which he'd thought he'd finally made peace.

But the truth was, she'd always had this effect on him, long before al Adar had attacked the embassy. The day he met her, he'd felt as if something in his world had shifted, knocked his life off its steady, predictable axis.

Everything had changed for him in Kaziristan, long before the embassy siege.

"So, we got sort of distracted before," she said a few minutes later, about halfway through the falafel wrap she was eating with gusto. Her obvious pleasure in the food, and the improvement of both her spirits and her physical strength, came as a huge relief to Darcy.

"Yes, we did." And if he let himself focus on recalling the details of that distraction, he might end up throwing caution to the wind and going for another round.

"You didn't tell me how your talk with Ava went."

"Right." Nothing quite like the memory of his frustrating trip to The Gates to pour cold water on his reawakening libido. "It went fine, I guess. Her assessment of Cade Landry seemed to fit what you told me about him. She also had some interesting thoughts about the head of the Johnson City RA, Pete Chang." He told her what Ava had said about Chang's brownnosing habits.

She grimaced. "The sort who'll lick any boot on the ladder rungs above him?"

"Seems to be the case."

"Federal agencies are just chock-full of Pete Changs." She sat back in her chair, folding her hands over her stomach. "So if someone up the chain of command had asked him to sabotage my case—"

"He might have, especially if he's not the sort to question orders."

Her eyes narrowed. "But you don't think it's Chang."

"I don't think this feels like something that would come down the chain of command," he said. "It feels more—"

"Local," she finished for him.

He nodded. "I'd be looking at Knoxville or Johnson City if someone had put me in charge of this investigation."

"Someone *has* put you in charge," she said in a suddenly serious tone. "I have. I'm too close to the players to be objective."

"Are you?" he asked before he could stop himself.

Her brow furrowed. "Am I too close to be objective?"

"Are you close, period? To anyone. On the job or—?"

Her lips curved. "Isn't it a little late to be asking that question, Romeo?"

She had a point. They'd come bloody close to ripping off their clothes and having sex right there in the middle of the tiny kitchen. There was a part of him, fed by desire humming in his blood, that still wanted to give it a go.

"Are you involved with someone in Knoxville? Someone who might start looking for you?"

"No. I haven't had much time to date. I work a lot." She pushed her fingers through her unruly hair, once again managing to tame the wild curls, gentling them with her touch. A fresh surge of desire washed through him, and he struggled not to reach across the table for her.

"What about your family?"

"There's just my mom. Dad died a couple of years ago."

A stab of sympathy sliced his chest. "I'm sorry. I hadn't heard."

"Cancer. Hit fast and, mercifully, he didn't suffer long." She released a long, slow breath. "Could have been a lot worse. There are so many worse ways to die."

The last of his appetite fled. He and McKenna had seen a whole lot of death up close and very personal eight years earlier. And it wasn't the last time he'd seen the fleeting nature of life or how cruel death could be.

"Do you think you were followed back here?" she asked after a few long moments of uncomfortable silence.

He covered the remainder of his falafel wrap with the foil and put it back in the bag. "I don't think so. I think if I had been, someone would have already made a move on us."

She wrapped up her own leftovers and added them to the bag. "I think I'll save the baklava for later."

He reached across the table and caught her hand as she reached for the sticky dessert. "I'm going to protect you. Whatever it takes. You know that, don't you?"

"I'm an FBI agent. I don't need you to protect me." She lifted her chin. "But I know you'll have my back. And that means a lot."

"You'll have mine, too." He threaded his fingers through hers, giving them a light squeeze before letting go. "I need a shower. And we both could use some sleep."

"You go ahead. I'll clean up." She put the baklava back in the bag and headed toward the refrigerator.

In the bathroom, he stripped off his shirt and stopped short, his gaze snagged by his own reflection in the mirror. He looked rough. There was really no other word for it. His hair needed a trim, he hadn't shaved in a couple of days and he'd lost weight since joining The Gates, his natural bulk carved down to an almost feral leanness.

But he was stronger than he'd ever been. In better shape. And until that weak moment earlier in the kitchen, he'd been as clearheaded as he could remember being.

He was a different man from the Nicholas Darcy who'd worked in a suit and tie, playing by the State Department rules and living the same familiar life of embassies and receptions and protocol that he'd known since he was old enough to have a lucid memory.

But which man did he want to be?

The one who gets to kiss McKenna Rigsby whenever he wants.

Closing his eyes against the treacherous thought, he finished undressing and turned on the shower tap, adjusting the water to cool.

Bracing himself, he stepped under the cold spray.

WHILE DARCY SHOWERED, McKenna wandered around the small cabin, familiarizing herself with the place. It was just the big front room, a single bedroom, the kitchen and the bathroom, where Darcy was naked under a steamy shower, naked as the day he was born—

Focus, Rigsby.

What she needed was a computer and an internet connection. She'd ditched her phone once she realized she was up against someone in the FBI. Too easy to locate her by GPS, so she'd tossed the phone in a creek several miles back, hoping the water would render the damned thing useless. And even if it didn't, the FBI could track her only as far as the creek.

But she felt closed off from the world outside without her phone.

She smelled Darcy before she heard his footsteps, a clean, soapy scent mixed with something darker and more masculine. She turned and found him leaning against the bedroom door frame, his eyes narrowing slightly as her gaze met his.

"You're supposed to be resting." He softened his stern words with a faint smile.

"I'm not tired."

He'd shaved, she noticed. The lack of facial hair didn't temper the edginess she'd noticed right away when her fuzzy mind had cleared and she'd been able to take in the full impact of the man he'd become.

Age had made him leaner. Harder. But in a good way. He looked stronger. Fiercer.

He looked like a warrior.

"Then maybe we should sit down and go back over the details of your undercover assignment again. After I check your bandages." He backed out of the bedroom doorway, gesturing down the hall with his hand.

She followed him to the front room and settled on the sofa, grimacing as he sat on the footlocker and reached for the first-aid kit still sitting there from earlier that day. "It's not even really hurting."

"Good. Maybe we've got the infection on the run. But that's no reason to stop doing what's working, is it?"

She could hardly argue with such logic, so she lifted the edge of her T-shirt and turned her body toward him. "How does it look?" she asked as he eased the gauze and tape away from her wounds.

"Better, actually." He tore open a couple of antiseptic wipes and dabbed at the two holes in her side. "Sorry," he added quickly when she sucked in a sharp breath at the sting.

"It's okay. Doesn't hurt nearly as much as it did this morning."

"The inflammation appears to be receding." Finished with the cleaning, he applied more antiseptic, then soothed the renewed sting with the cool relief of aloe vera gel. A quick application of gauze and tape later, he sat back. "All done."

"Thanks." She felt shivery all over, and she knew it wasn't due to the pain of her injury. She needed to concentrate on figuring out what the BRI and their friend at the FBI were really up to and stop letting Darcy's proximity get to her.

They had a lead, didn't they? Cade Landry was as good a place to start as any.

"I want to look a little closer at Cade Landry," Darcy said before she could speak.

"I was just thinking the same thing."

"When I spoke to Ava, she said the man was on the fast track up the career ladder at the bureau for the early part of his career. But a year or so ago, something changed, and he was on a downward spiral, careerwise. She didn't know what that something was."

A memory twitched in the back of her mind. Something about an operation gone wrong. "Did Ava know where he was working before he was transferred to Johnson City?"

"I think she said Richmond."

The twitch got stronger. "There was a domestic terror investigation that went very wrong a little over a year ago. FBI agents had tracked a couple of bombing suspects to a warehouse. There were civilians inside and they were threatening to blow them all up."

Darcy nodded. "I remember that."

"According to FBI scuttlebutt, after SWAT arrived, the order came to hold position until the negotiation unit could get there."

He nodded. "Standard protocol."

"Right. But for some reason, one SWAT unit ignored the order and went in. Two members of the team and eight civilians were killed when one of the suspects detonated his bomb. Dozens of others were injured, including the rest of the SWAT unit that disobeyed orders."

Darcy was looking at her with a frown. "Hmm."

"What?"

He leaned closer. "When I was talking to Ava earlier, there was another agent in the office. And when I mentioned Cade Landry's name, that agent dropped a stack of files."

"And that's significant because…?"

"She was an FBI agent before taking the job at The Gates a few months ago. I remember Quinn saying she'd felt the FBI was a dead end for her and she was looking for new opportunities."

"I imagine for anyone who had been part of that unit that disobeyed orders, the FBI was probably a dead end," she said, finally following what he was saying. "You think Landry was part of the unit that blew the call, right? And your friend at The Gates might have been on the same team, too?"

"It's pure speculation at this point."

"But speculation worth investigating." She stood, driven by the need to do something besides hide in this cabin, living in fear of discovery.

Darcy rose with her, his brow furrowed. "You're supposed to be resting while I do the investigating."

"I'm fine. Most of my strength is back now."

"Really? Clasp your hands behind your back."

The mere thought made her wince.

"My point exactly."

The hint of triumph in Darcy's dark eyes annoyed her into action. "I don't need to put my hands behind my back to investigate." Dodging him, she grabbed her Glock from the coffee table and attached the holster to the front waistband of her jeans. The holster was meant to fit in the small of her back, but as Darcy had so annoyingly proved, reaching behind her back wasn't a good idea if she wanted to be fast on the draw.

She sat on the footlocker and picked up the tennis shoes she'd kicked off earlier, ignoring the hot pain lancing through her side at the exertion.

"Where exactly are you going to go?" Darcy asked, his tone dark with irritation. "You're in the middle of nowhere and you don't even know how to get out of here."

"You said hike north to get to Quinn's place, right?"

"You're going to Quinn?"

"You said he wants you to keep me safe. What's he going to do, turn me in to the FBI?" She grimaced as the pain in her side seemed to translate to fumble fingers. She couldn't seem to get the shoestrings to cooperate.

Darcy crouched at her feet, gently moving her hands aside and making quick work of the laces. He looked up at her, his expression a curious blend of annoyance and admiration. "It's at least two miles. Uphill most of the way. If you're determined to go see Quinn, I can take you in the Land Rover, but I think you need to seriously consider the consequences if you're wrong about what he'll do."

"What am I supposed to do? Sit here and wait for someone to finally track me down?" To her dismay, she felt tears burning her eyes. She blinked them away fiercely, determined not to show weakness. "Someone set me up, made me look like a traitor. Someone *shot* me, for God's sake. I don't think they were shooting to miss."

"I don't, either," he agreed, his voice rough. Remaining crouched before her, he took her hands in his. "But they haven't gone away. They're still out there looking for you, and you don't know which ones wish merely to bring you in for interrogation and which ones want you dead."

She looked down at their entwined hands. "I know."

"I really thought I'd never see you again." His voice dropped to a raspy whisper. "I'd run into people who'd seen you, and if I was brave, I'd even ask about you. But I never let myself go beyond the basics. I never asked if you'd met someone, if you'd married, if you were a mother now—" She heard an odd timbre to his voice, a hint of regret.

She couldn't stop herself from touching his face. "I didn't. I haven't. I'm not."

He curved his cheek into her touch, his eyes closing. "I shouldn't be glad about that."

Her heart pounding beneath her breastbone, she cradled his face between her hands, drawing him closer. "I shouldn't be, either. But I am."

Closing the distance between them, she kissed him.

Chapter Eleven

One hot summer night in Tablis, Darcy had gone for a swim in the embassy pool. Technically, anyone employed by the embassy could swim in the Olympic-size pool behind the embassy's fortified walls, but by custom, the daylight hours were left to the diplomats and their families, while the support staff, including the FBI's legat staff and the security personnel, waited until evening hours, if they were lucky enough to be off duty.

After ten in the evening was the best time if a person preferred to swim alone, Darcy had discovered. Most of the staff had gone to bed by then, leaving him alone to get in his laps and work off the day's stresses before bedtime.

But that hot summer night, he had not been alone. A young woman with a lithe, muscular shape had been cutting waves through the pool's clear water, powering her way from end to end as if racing a clock. He'd recognized her—barely—as the new legat agent.

She'd pulled up short as she reached the end where Darcy stood, water streaming from her chaos of curls and sliding with sensuous leisure over the curves of her breasts, so chastely but inadequately hidden beneath the modest one-piece bathing suit. Moonlight brought out deep auburn glimmers in her damp hair and cast her fair skin with a pearly glow that reminded Darcy of a Waterhouse painting he'd seen once at an art gallery in England, depicting young Hylas enchanted by naiads.

Brushing the water away from her eyes, his late-night intruder had offered a sweet smile worthy of those other-worldly water nymphs and apologized. "I thought I'd be alone at this hour."

It had been McKenna Rigsby's first day at the embassy, and Darcy had been utterly enchanted.

Getting involved with her romantically had been out of the question, of course. Tensions in Kaziristan kept all embassy personnel on alert, leaving them little time for anything but the most cursory of friendships. And they'd both worked high-stress, dangerous jobs that allowed no room for distractions.

Like kissing each other until they were utterly breathless.

She tugged him closer, her arms wrapping around his neck until she pulled his chest flush against hers. Her pulse raced in tandem with his as she parted her lips, inviting him to deepen the kiss.

Maybe she really was a naiad, he thought as her hair tangled around his hands, ensnaring him until he felt as though he was becoming part of her, helpless to resist her spell.

But he had to resist. This day, eight years later, was no less dangerous than that night at the US Embassy in Tablis. The enemy had changed, but terror was still afoot. People's lives were still in grave peril.

And as before, McKenna and Darcy stood in the breach, trying to keep death at bay.

He dragged his mouth away from hers, trying to catch his breath again. "We can't do this."

"I know," she murmured, reaching for him again.

Catching her hands, he held them together between his own to keep them still. "We can't do this, McKenna. Not now. For the same reasons as before. You know that."

She closed her eyes and leaned back. "Damn it."

"We need to keep our minds clear. We have to be able to function as a professional team. We've already lost precious time while you've been recuperating. It's not your fault," he added quickly at her stricken look, "but it's just the way things are. We're behind and we don't even know what the Blue Ridge Infantry might be planning. Do we?"

She shook her head. "I know it's big and it's going to be deadly. That's their goal. But I don't know what they have planned."

"Or who in the FBI is working with them."

"Right." She tugged her hands away from his, her composure back in place. She tamed her hair with steady hands and met his gaze with a look of raw determination. "I think we need to start with the second question first. Who is aiding the BRI in their plans? We have our suspicions about Cade Landry, right?"

He nodded. "But I don't want to get so focused on him that we drop the ball and fail to look at other suspects."

"I've known Glen Robertson for several years, even before I was transferred to the Knoxville Field Office." Her gaze followed him as he rose to his feet in front of her. "I can't imagine him doing anything that wasn't completely honorable."

"People can deceive you."

"I know that. I'm not naive."

"I know you're not." His voice softened. "Instead of going to talk to Quinn, why don't we go back to my cabin for now? Anyone who was looking for you in that area has probably moved on by now. And I have internet."

"We should probably wait until night."

He nodded. "Safer that way." He crossed to the doorway and grabbed his leather jacket from the garment hook nailed to the cabin's rough wood walls. "I'll be back."

She rose. "Where are you going?"

"To check the Land Rover. Make sure nobody has tampered with it. I'll knock four times fast and twice slow so you'll know I'm the one at the door and won't shoot me." Flashing her a smile, he lifted the collar of his jacket against the brisk April breeze as he stepped out onto the creaking porch, welcoming the dose of cold to help him get his simmering libido back under control.

The Land Rover was where he'd parked after returning from his roundabout tour of mountain roads in an attempt to shake the vehicles that had been following him. All four tires looked to be intact, and a careful check of the chassis and under the hood convinced him he hadn't picked up any trackers or other sort of electronic parasites.

He'd gassed up once he felt certain he'd lost the tail, so they should be good for the trip to his cabin on Killshadow Road.

When he got back to the cabin, he knocked using the code he'd told her to listen for. No gun pointed his way when he entered again. In fact, McKenna wasn't in the front room at all.

"Rigsby?" he called.

"Back here."

He followed the sound of her voice and found her in the bedroom, packing things back into his duffel bag. "I see you're ready to be gone."

She shot him a wry smile. "You had me at *internet.*"

They cleaned up the cabin before they left, trying to put everything back the way it had been. Darcy stuffed their used linens and towels in a garbage bag he found under the kitchen cabinet. "I can launder them at my place and bring them back before Bragg and Susannah return," he told McKenna as she eyed the bag.

She fluffed the bed pillows and stood back to survey her

handiwork. "They'll know we were here when they find the extra food in the cabinets."

"Nobody ever complains about intruders who leave gifts."

She sighed, dropping onto the edge of the bed. "I don't know how I ended up here, in a situation like this. My career was my life."

Well aware he was playing with fire, he sat beside her on the bed. "I know the feeling."

"What happened to you, Darcy?" She twisted to look at him, a brief frown the only sign that the movement caused her any pain.

She *was* getting better, he thought.

"I stopped playing by the rules," he answered.

"That's cryptic."

"After Kaziristan, I saw how Barton Reid twisted everything I believed in to turn Maddox Heller into a scapegoat." He frowned at the memory of the sick, sinking feeling that had twisted his gut when he'd heard how Reid and his sycophants at Foggy Bottom had destroyed the good name of a brave, honorable Marine. "We were there, Rigsby. We saw how it happened."

"He saved our lives. He saved everyone but Teresa."

"We didn't know at the time how deeply indebted to the militants Reid had become."

"The bureau was only tangentially involved in the investigation of Reid," she said. "But I know enough to know he was corrupt to the bone."

"I helped bring him down."

She arched one ginger eyebrow at him. "That didn't make the papers."

"I guess, to be more accurate, I should say I helped the people who brought him down."

"Cooper Security, right?"

He nodded, remembering that night in Washington, DC,

when he'd gotten the call from Alexander Quinn asking for his help. He'd been inclined to ignore the call from Quinn—in his experience, cooperating with Quinn was rarely a good idea.

"Quinn called me. Told me a man named Jesse Cooper was on his way to Washington with a woman who was in grave danger from elements within the government who wanted to use her as leverage against her father."

"Her father?"

"Baxter Marsh." He saw the recognition dawn. "Yes, the same Baxter Marsh who headed the Marine Corps' part of the joint task force in Kaziristan."

"Reid was trying to get his hands on some coded journal, right?"

He nodded. "Jesse Cooper had the journal. They'd managed to decode the journal using the three keys General Marsh and his two fellow generals had created."

"Right. I remember that part of the story. Each man had entrusted the key to one other person, in case something happened to one of them, right?"

"Yes. And something did happen to one of them. General Ross died in a suspicious car crash. But he'd hidden his part of the key in a locket he gave his wife. So, eventually, his key was added to the other two keys to decode the journal and reveal the secrets that brought Barton Reid down."

"Along with several people in the previous administration," she said bluntly. "And you helped Cooper get his hands on that information?"

"I did. I also used my friendship with the British ambassador to the US to get Cooper and Evie Marsh into a big reception at the embassy."

"No wonder you hit a ceiling on the job."

He looked at her through narrowed eyes. "Do you think I did the wrong thing?"

She shook her head quickly. "Bad people got caught and put away. Wasn't that your job?"

He couldn't quell a smile. "Something like that."

"Then good for you, Nicholas Darcy. You didn't let the rules get in the way of doing the right thing." Her smile in return felt like the warm sun breaking through clouds on a cold day.

They made sandwiches for dinner and ate them on the winding drive back to Darcy's cabin. He watched carefully for any sign of a tail, but if there was anyone following them back to Killshadow Road, they were invisible in the darkness.

After an hour-long trip that took fifty minutes longer than the journey would normally take, he parked the Land Rover on the gravel drive in front of the cabin and cut the engine. "Wait here," he said. "And stay alert."

The cabin was dark and looked undisturbed, but that didn't mean anything when one was dealing with the FBI. He opened the Land Rover's back hatch and pulled out the toolbox he had stored there.

"What are you doing?" McKenna turned to watch him.

"Looking for this." He pulled out the small detection device that had come with the job at The Gates. Quinn had warned him that working for an agency that dealt with the sort of cases The Gates handled automatically made them all targets by enemies both domestic and foreign.

"You need to know if someone's listening," Quinn had warned him as he handed him the device.

Now he turned on the bug sniffer and headed up the porch steps, watching the little device do its work.

After covering the entire cabin without receiving any warning blips, he pocketed the sniffer and went back out to the Land Rover. "We're good."

McKenna climbed out of the Land Rover, moving a little more slowly than she had earlier in the day. She'd exerted herself more that day than she had since her injury, and the extra exercise was clearly starting to take a toll.

"Go straight to bed," he ordered. "I'll lock up."

She stared at him. "Are you crazy? It's not even nine o'clock. Just point me to your computer and I promise I'll sit still while I'm surfing the Net. We've already wasted more time than I like."

He decided not to argue for once. She was right. They were already behind, and time was running out.

"It's in my bedroom."

She started down the hall, then stopped, looking back at him. "What's the username and password?"

He froze in place. "Username is just my last name."

"And the password?"

Heat bloomed in his neck and cheeks as he realized he'd just stepped into a minefield.

"Darcy?" she said when he didn't answer right away.

He took a deep breath and got it over with. "It's Mc-Kenna, backward with no capital letters."

She stared at him a moment, her eyes luminous. "Oh, Darcy."

"*Tempus fugit*, Rigsby," he said gruffly, tapping his watch. "Time flies."

She flashed him a bright smile and disappeared down the hallway.

He glanced at his watch. Just after seven. There was a chance someone was still in the office, he knew. The normal hours at The Gates were eight to five, but none of the agents kept normal hours.

He'd worked deep into the evening several times himself. So it was possible Olivia Sharp was still in the office, wasn't it?

He pulled his cell phone from his pocket and dialed the direct number to the agents' bull pen. On the third ring, Cain Dennison's gravelly drawl answered, "The Gates."

"You're there late, Dennison. Sara out on the town with the girls?"

"If by 'out on the town with the girls' you mean on a stakeout over in Bitterwood, then yes. Yes, she is." The humorous tone of his voice didn't quite mask his wariness. "I heard you were in the office today."

"I was. Needed to pick Ava Trent's brain about something."

"Anything to do with why you're staying at Bragg's cabin?"

"No," Darcy lied. "Just following up on something. Is Olivia Sharp in the office by any chance?"

"Just missed her. She left around twenty minutes ago."

"Oh, okay. I'll talk to you later."

"Wait, Darcy."

The urgent edge to Dennison's voice made him do as the other man asked. "What is it?"

"Are you sure you're okay? You know if you need anything, all you have to do is call."

Darcy felt a niggle of guilt. "I know. I do. I'm fine."

"Okay." Dennison sounded unconvinced. "You know where to reach me if that changes."

The differences between Dennison and Darcy might outweigh the similarities, but Darcy believed him. If he ended up needing help, Dennison would come through for him.

It was gratifying to know he wasn't nearly as alone as he'd felt the past few years. "Thank you. I'll keep that in mind."

He hung up the phone and shoved it back in his pocket, wondering if he was going to have to take Dennison up on the offer before this case was over.

SHE WAS HIS PASSWORD.

As far as McKenna knew, she'd never been anyone's

password before. And Darcy's, of all the buttoned-up, unromantic souls in the universe…

"Grow up, Rigsby," she muttered as she powered up the laptop and waited for the log-in screen. But the corners of her lips still twitched at the thought of Darcy still thinking enough of her, all these years later, to use her name as a password.

She logged in, pulled up a browser window and typed in the name Cade Landry. Within seconds, she had pages full of Cade Landrys, so she narrowed the search by adding "FBI" to the parameters.

The entries narrowed down considerably. And most of them were about the explosion near Richmond.

As she clicked through the link to the first entry, she heard Darcy's footsteps coming down the hall. A moment later, his voice rumbled from the doorway. "Any luck?"

"Just got started." She patted the edge of the bed next to her and began scanning the online article. It was a pretty straightforward report of the incident and the injuries and deaths involved. Landry was one of the FBI agents mentioned. "If I was still able to access anything from the FBI database—but they cut me off."

"I'm cut off from most of the resources we have available at The Gates, too." He sat next to her. "Rather inconvenient, that."

She slanted a look at him. "You don't think that one has anything to do with the other, do you? You said you and your agency have been trying to dismantle the BRI and their affiliates—and the BRI is certainly part of what's happened to me…"

"I don't see how the two cases could be connected, though," he said thoughtfully. "I don't see how people would have linked you to me, or vice versa. We haven't spoken in years, and I doubt anyone in the BRI would have been at the American Embassy in Kaziristan nearly a decade ago."

She nodded, looking back at the computer screen. "It wouldn't have mattered if they were. We were always very careful not to let anything between us show. To anyone."

"Ourselves included."

He was so solid beside her. So strong and warm. The urge to curl up against his side felt like a physical craving.

She controlled the desire and clicked on another link. "We had our reasons."

The story in the second link looked to be longer and more substantial, she noted. It was dated a couple of days after the explosion, when both investigators and journalists would have had time to eliminate most of the misinformation and fill in the blanks of the story.

The tone of the story was much more critical of the FBI, of course. By that time, word of the botched standoff would have reached the ears of someone in the news business. Too many people in the bureau were happy to throw another agent or two under the bus in order to make themselves look good in comparison.

Cade Landry's name came up. Often. But it was a name near the middle of the page that caught her eye. "Well, would you look at that?"

Darcy leaned closer, the heat of him enveloping her with delicious warmth. "What?"

She pointed to the screen. "Look what group authorities believed the two bombers belonged to."

Darcy uttered a short profanity. "The Blue Ridge Infantry."

Chapter Twelve

Darcy had finally coaxed McKenna to bed around eleven the night before, but he'd stayed up a little longer, hunting down all the references he could find to the connection between the Blue Ridge Infantry and the two bombers involved in the Richmond incident that had cost Cade Landry his fast track up the FBI ladder.

Ava Solano had told him that Landry seemed to be apathetic about his job these days, but was apathy hiding something else? What if Landry had been involved with the Blue Ridge Infantry all along? What if the botched raid had been an attempt to help his comrades escape? The bomb detonation could have been accidental—all it would have taken was a nervous militia member with a twitchy trigger finger to set off a bomb belt.

Landry definitely deserved greater scrutiny, he decided the next morning when he headed to the kitchen to start a pot of coffee. And getting in contact with Olivia Sharp was the first place to start.

The aroma of freshly brewed coffee hit him halfway to the kitchen. He found McKenna at the table, sipping coffee and reading another article on his laptop computer.

"Grab some coffee," she invited with a cheeky grin. "Or maybe you could whip us up an omelet. I'm starving."

"You look a lot better."

"I feel a lot better." She stretched her arms over her head, not even wincing. "I slept like a log."

He could tell. She looked rested and beautiful. "Good. It seems to have done you a world of good."

"So, what's on our agenda this morning?" she asked as he crossed to the refrigerator for eggs.

"Breakfast," he said. "Then you can continue your internet research while I drive into town to track down Olivia Sharp."

McKenna turned from the laptop to look at him. "Right. She works at The Gates now, you said."

He put a skillet on the stove to heat while he stirred eggs, cheese, milk and spices together for the omelet. "I don't know her well. She came to work there shortly before I was put on administrative leave. But I'm hoping she'll be willing to answer a few questions for me about the incident in Richmond."

"And about Cade Landry?"

"Exactly."

"Well, do me a favor, will you? If you talk to her, ask her who the incident commander for her unit was. So far, all the news accounts keep referring to him by his job title. Not one has mentioned him by name."

He finished pouring the omelet mixture into the pan before he turned to look at her. "That's odd, I take it?"

"Very odd. I don't know why nobody supplied his name to the news outlets. They had no trouble naming any of the other agents on that team."

He dished up their omelets and set the plates on the table, taking his own seat opposite her. "Put away the laptop and eat."

With a sigh that reminded him of her workaholic days at the embassy, she slid the laptop to the side and picked up her fork. "Remember when we sneaked into the embassy kitchen in the middle of the night to make scrambled eggs for everybody getting off guard duty for the night?"

He smiled at the memory. "You always did know how to get people in trouble."

"How was I supposed to know the eggs were for some VIP brunch the next morning?" She took a bite of the omelet. "You still have the touch."

"I think it's just that you have the palate of a culinary philistine," he said, affecting his most plummy accent.

"Snob." She pointed her fork at him. "It is a truth universally acknowledged that a single man in possession of a good omelet must be in want of a wife."

"Nice. Paraphrasing Jane Austen. Which actually makes you a dilettante not a philistine."

"Don't make me look that word up." She shot him a saucy grin that made him want to sweep the plates of omelets aside and have his way with her right there on the kitchen table.

"Rigsby, you're better educated than I am. Now, finish your spectacular omelet and stop trying to distract me with your smart mouth."

He made quick work of his own omelet, moved his plate aside and slid the laptop computer in front of him. "Have you started looking into the backgrounds of any of the other agents on the suspect list?"

"Not since I found the articles on the Richmond bomb case." She stopped about two-thirds of the way through her omelet, pushing the plate aside. "Ugh, stuffed. You want the rest?"

He eyed the leftovers. "Since when do you leave food on the plate, Rigsby? Are you feeling okay?"

"I'm fine. I just—" Her reluctant tone made him look up. She was frowning, her earlier good mood gone.

"What's wrong?"

"I was just thinking about the past couple of weeks. Those men in the BRI aren't misunderstood. They're not mistaken or misled. They're cruel, chauvinistic bastards. They treat their women like property, to use or abuse as they see fit."

Something in her eyes made his chest ache. "What exactly was your role in this undercover operation, McKenna?"

"They have what I suppose you'd call 'groupies.' Women who like the mystique of their pseudo patriotism. You know, I've investigated other militia groups. Some of them aren't bad people. They just take individual freedom very seriously and worry about the encroachment of the federal government on matters that should be private or local. And I get that, Darcy. I do. I grew up in the mountains where federal programs have left whole generations of people on the draw. That's what we called it. The monthly welfare payments people draw. That's what happens when you let the government try to fix all your problems for you. But the BRI—they're just playing at that kind of 'don't tread on me' sensibility. They don't mean it. They want something else altogether."

The pain in her voice caught him by surprise. She'd talked about her North Carolina childhood quite a bit during their time together at the embassy, but most of the stories had been happy memories.

"What was your role?" he prodded, more gently this time.

She toyed with her fork. "I was supposed to befriend the groupies. Try to work my way into the perimeter of the group that way."

"You're not groupie material."

She smiled at that, and he felt some of the tightness in

his chest ease. "No, I'm not. But I was the only woman on the task force, so I got tapped anyway."

"How far inside did you get?" he asked, not certain he wanted to hear the answer.

"Not far," she said quickly, her gaze darting up to meet his. "Not far at all. They're very suspicious of outsiders. And I may have the right kind of accent, but this is a group of people who know everyone they're dealing with. The bureau tried to set me up with a backstory that would be convincing, but I think they sometimes forget that the BRI isn't just another backyard militia. They've been working hand in glove with some very bright computer geeks for a few years now."

"And someone saw through your cover story?"

"I don't think it was that, exactly," she admitted. "They weren't going to let me into the inner circle if they couldn't go deeper into my background, though. That much was pretty clear fairly soon."

"You told me before someone in the FBI found out you'd gotten close to putting something together on the BRI. How, if they wouldn't let you into the inner circle?"

"What I learned wasn't from the BRI. It was from one of the anarchists." A smile flirted with the corners of her mouth. "He was young. And hot for me. He wasn't particularly subtle about it, either. And I realized maybe there was more than one way to get the information I wanted. But—" Her smile faded, and she looked down at her hands.

Darcy leaned toward her, touching the back of her hand with his fingertips, his gut twisting with sudden alarm. "But?"

"He wanted sex. I wasn't going to give it to him. Definitely not in my job description." She turned her hand over, her fingers brushing lightly against his. Once, twice. Then she pulled her hands into her lap. "He got violent. I had to take him down, and after that, they looked a hell of a lot more closely at me, I guess."

"Is that when you overheard people talking about the Fibber?"

She nodded. "I had to sneak a lot at that point. People would clam up if they saw me coming. Honestly, I'm not sure why they didn't just kill me at that point. Maybe they thought I'd be useful in another way. Maybe by feeding me misinformation about what they were up to."

"How can you be sure they're up to something at all, then?" Darcy sat back, searching her face for any sign she was keeping something from him. It wasn't that he thought she'd intentionally mislead him about something important regarding the case they were investigating.

But maybe she'd keep to herself anything that happened to her when she was vulnerable and alone in a den of vipers like the BRI.

Was there something she wasn't telling him?

"You think I'm lying?" Her eyes narrowed in response. He should have known she'd see through his attempt to cover his doubts.

"I think maybe something happened with the BRI that you're not telling me. Did someone—?" His throat closed up before he finished asking the question.

She leaned forward suddenly, reaching across the table to close her hand over his. "No, Darcy. No. Nothing like that happened. I promise you."

He saw the truth in her eyes and felt his muscles relax, just a little.

She stroked the back of his hand with her thumb. "I know they're up to something because Ax let that much slip before I had to pull my best judo moves on him."

Darcy arched one eyebrow. "Ax?"

"It was his nickname, I'm sure. He never told me his real name. The BRI seem to go by their real names, but their anarchist buddies are all about the pseudonyms." She started to withdraw her hand, but he caught it, twining his fingers with hers. She looked up at him, her sharp green eyes softening. "I think he was trying to impress me."

"Are you sure it was the truth?"

"He tried to backtrack once I had him on the ground. Said he was just making things up."

"But you didn't believe him?'

"No. I'm pretty good at figuring out when someone's lying or telling the truth." She let go of his hand. "If you're going to catch up with Olivia Sharp, you should probably get a move on."

He couldn't tell if she was trying to deflect him from her experiences with the BRI or if she was simply eager for him to see what Olivia had to say about Cade Landry.

Either way, she was right. The earlier he showed up at The Gates, the more likely he'd catch Olivia Sharp on her way in or out of the office.

"Mr. Darcy has a concussion, but he's not showing any signs of a more dangerous injury." The military doctor looked tired and harried, his tone clipped but his eyes kind as he paused in the triage waiting area to update the ragtag handful of embassy security personnel who'd gathered to get information on their fallen comrades. "He's asking for someone named Rigsby?"

All eyes turned to McKenna. She felt heat rising in her cheeks.

"You can see him for a few minutes, but don't stay long. There's a lot going on in the triage area, as I'm sure you can imagine." The doctor nodded toward the door leading into the base's busy medical unit. "He's in bay number four."

Ignoring the curious looks of the other agents, McKenna entered the triage unit and followed the signs to exam bay four, where she found Darcy resting on a gurney. His eyes were closed, and his face looked pale and haggard. But when she moved closer, he opened his eyes and managed a halfhearted smile. "Good. You're here. I need a lawyer."

She moved closer, her fingers brushing the sheet beside his hand, allowing herself the ambient warmth but not the actual touch of skin to skin. She felt too vulnerable at the moment to trust herself. "You need a lawyer?"

"They're keeping me in this bloody hospital against my will," he grumbled, his dark eyes soft and persuasive as he gazed at her beneath the gauze bandage over his wounded head. "File a motion or something."

Relief fluttered through her. If he was well enough to complain, he was in better condition than she'd feared. "I have a better idea. Listen to what your doctors tell you to do. And do it."

He grimaced. "I was really counting on your rule-breaking tendencies, Rigsby. You've let me down."

Her knees felt wobbly, but there was nowhere to sit except the edge of the gurney. And she'd be damned if she'd do something so intimate with dozens of military doctors moving from patient to patient behind her. She found the steel in her spine and managed a smile, though she could feel the hot sting of tears at the backs of her eyes. "They'll let you out as soon as they think you're out of the woods. I should let you rest."

As she started to back away, Darcy's hand snaked out to circle her wrist. "Cameron?"

She shook her head, blinking back guilty tears.

"I'm sorry." He released her hand. "What about Jamil and the others in the kitchen?"

"Jamil is okay. He sustained some minor burns and a broken arm. Rafik is in surgery for a ruptured spleen. They haven't found Yusef. They're not sure if he was blown

clear of the kitchen by the rocket fire and managed to walk away or..."

"Or al Adar captured him." Darcy grimaced. He knew as well as she did what the terrorists did to "collaborators."

"Darcy, you need to rest."

"They're transferring me stateside as soon as they release me."

The twisting pain in her gut caught her by surprise. "So soon?"

He nodded, holding her gaze with his fathomless brown eyes. "I don't know where I'll be reassigned."

So this is goodbye, *she thought, seeing the truth in his troubled gaze.* "I'll be sticking around for a while. The bureau wants those of us who survived to help the incident investigation team."

He nodded, wincing a little at the movement. "That's why I wanted to talk to you. Because I don't think I'll see you again after this. We both know you won't try to look me up. Will you?"

The finality hit her like a body blow. Appearances be damned, she sat on the edge of the gurney before her legs gave out. "No. I won't," she admitted, hating herself. Hating him. And wishing they were different people in a different place at a different time.

"I don't think I would have survived the siege without you, Rigsby." He brushed the back of her hand with his fingertips. "Thank you."

She was not going to cry. She wasn't.

"Don't let the bureau break you. They'll try. They always do."

"I won't." Tears burned the backs of her eyes but she didn't let them spill. She couldn't.

Not while Darcy was watching.

McKenna woke with a start, her heart thudding heavily against her rib cage. Blinking away the sleep, she checked her watch. Only thirty minutes had passed since Darcy walked out the door. He'd told her as he left not to worry unless she didn't hear from him in a couple of hours.

Then she was supposed to call Alexander Quinn.

She rubbed her eyes, surprised to find tears dampening the skin beneath them. She'd been dreaming, she remembered. About that last day with Darcy at the base hospital outside Tablis.

Saying goodbye.

She knuckled away the tears and sat up from the sofa, eyeing the laptop she'd set on the coffee table before stretching out to rest her eyes. Her life was in danger. Her reputation as an FBI agent in tatters. It would be so easy to give up, to just hunker down and wait for everything to unfold. Sooner or later, the BRI would strike and everything she tried to warn people about would come to pass.

But she wasn't the kind of person who could sit back and let people die if she could stop it.

It was time to get back to work.

As she opened the laptop, she heard the thud of footsteps on the porch outside. She barely had time to grab her Glock when she heard the hard scrape of metal on metal and the door began to open.

She whipped the Glock up and brought it to bear on the broad-shouldered man who stepped through the door. The morning light poured in behind him, rendering him little more than a silhouette in the bright rectangle of the open doorway.

"Don't move," she commanded.

"Wouldn't dream of it," a familiar voice replied, his baritone tinged with amusement.

Son of a bitch.

"Nice to see you again, Agent Rigsby," Alexander Quinn said.

"Why do you want to know about Richmond?" Olivia Sharp crossed her legs, showing off an impressive golden tan and well-toned thigh muscles. She had an easy sensuality about her that reminded Darcy of a CIA agent he'd known back in Tablis. Tara Brady had worn her sexuality like armor, hiding the vulnerable woman underneath. Darcy had a feeling Olivia Sharp was not so different.

"I'm investigating the possibility that there's an FBI turncoat aiding the Blue Ridge Infantry." Darcy didn't see much point in lying.

"Investigating?" One honey-brown eyebrow arched delicately. "I thought you were on suspension."

"It's a personal project."

"What led you to me?"

"Cade Landry."

She flinched. It was only a slight twitch, but Darcy had been watching for any shift in her expression. She schooled her features immediately, her expression settling quickly back to neutral.

But she'd already given herself away.

"I worked with him," she said a second later.

"You both were involved in the botched raid."

Her jaw muscle twitched. "There was a miscommunication."

"Landry led your unit into the warehouse against orders."

"He said he received an order to go in."

"You didn't hear the order?"

Her eyes narrowed a notch. "I don't remember very much about the incident. I sustained a concussion from flying debris after the bomb detonation. I've never been able to remember the moments directly preceding or directly after the bombing."

He decided she was telling the truth, mostly because

he could see a hint of turmoil in those cool blue eyes. She didn't like not remembering what had really happened.

"How many people were in your unit?" he asked.

"Four, plus the unit commander, who wasn't directly on scene."

"Names?"

Her eyes iced over. "Why?"

"I told you. I think someone in the FBI might have been aiding the BRI members you had cornered in the warehouse."

"If so, he wasn't very good at it. One of the bombers blew himself up and the other was killed by sniper fire when he went for the detonator on his bomb belt."

That was new information, Darcy realized. "Sniper fire?"

"If he'd managed to set off the explosives belt, a lot more people would have died. The sniper made sure that didn't happen."

"Who were the members of the unit?"

"I was a member, of course. Cade Landry, as you know. We lost the other two members of the unit—Len Davis and Kevin Darnell. You must have seen their names in news reports if you've been looking into the incident."

He had, of course. Two FBI agents killed in the line of duty were big news. "And the unit commander?"

"I told you, he wasn't on the scene."

"No, I mean, who was he? What was his name?"

Her brow furrowed. "Are you testing me or something? If you've read the news reports, all of this information should have been in those articles."

"Most of it was," he admitted. "But not the name of the unit commander. He was even quoted. But not by name."

She looked genuinely puzzled. "Are you sure?"

"I'm certain. It's made me wonder how one manages to

head up an FBI operation that went entirely pear-shaped without his name being splashed across news accounts."

"I don't know," she admitted. "He has some decent connections in Congress. Enough that his career didn't go completely south." Her lips curved. "Though he himself went south."

"What does that mean?"

"I mean, he was transferred to a field office right here in Tennessee," Olivia answered. "He's a supervisory special agent in the Knoxville office. Darryl Boyle."

Chapter Thirteen

"You can put your weapon down, Rigsby. I'm unarmed."

McKenna didn't trust him, she realized. She'd talked big about going to Quinn earlier, but now she knew she'd have talked herself out of it. "I'll just hold on to this." She dropped the barrel away from him, however, waving him toward the armchair across from where she sat.

Quinn closed the door behind him and sat where she indicated. "You look well."

"I *am* well," she said firmly.

"You're favoring your left side," he said with a patient smile, crossing one leg over the other. "Subtle but there. You need to work on it if you want to convince anyone you're completely sound."

Alexander Quinn wasn't a tall man, nor particularly imposing. He had the sort of chameleon face that was perfect for spy work, she supposed. He could look very different from one day to the next with very little help from makeup or prosthetics.

Today, he looked like an ordinary, mild-mannered businessman in his midforties, his sandy hair touched with gray, his hazel eyes almost merry as he watched for her reaction.

"What do you want?"

"Darcy will protect you at all costs. Even from me. I assume you're aware of that fact or you'd never have come here looking for his help." Quinn's voice held a faint hint of the Appalachian accent that tinted the language of most people who lived here in the Smokies. McKenna's own drawl was far more pronounced, but she hadn't spent most of her life trying to hide her identity the way Quinn had.

"You're from mountain stock," she murmured. "From right here in eastern Tennessee. Aren't you?"

"I was born in Purgatory. Spent my first eighteen years here." His drawl broadened, as thick as her own. But with his next words, the accent was completely gone. "You were undercover for the FBI. Trying to infiltrate the Blue Ridge Infantry. Or, I should say, their legion of female admirers."

She didn't respond.

"You were unsuccessful."

"Can you get to your point?" she asked bluntly.

"I want to destroy the Blue Ridge Infantry. Root and branch."

"It sounds personal."

"It is" was his only response.

The sound of a vehicle approaching the cabin distracted McKenna for a split second, but that was enough for Quinn to reach behind his back and produce a big, black Ruger. "Stay here."

He was at the window next to the door within a couple of seconds, peering through the narrow space between the curtain and the wall. His tense posture eased marginally. "It's Darcy."

"He won't be happy to see you here," she warned.

Quinn flashed her a feral grin. "I know."

Darcy's footsteps sounded on the porch and stopped. Waited.

"He knows you're here," McKenna murmured.

"He knows someone besides you is here," Quinn corrected.

"Quinn?" Darcy's voice came from the other side of the door.

McKenna smiled. "He knows it's *you*. This is an Alexander Quinn stunt if ever there was one."

"Quinn, I'm coming in. Don't be armed." Though muffled by the door, there was no mistaking the commanding tone of Darcy's voice. McKenna saw that even Quinn arched an eyebrow at the sound.

"You gonna drop that Ruger or what?" she murmured, slanting him a sharp side-eye glance.

Quinn's lips pressed to a thin line, but he tucked the Ruger into the holster behind his back and stepped away from the door.

Darcy entered, his own weapon pulled. His gaze swept across McKenna, as if reassuring himself she was unharmed. Then he focused his intense gaze on Quinn.

"What the bloody hell are you doing here?"

"Checking on an old friend," Quinn answered, unperturbed.

"*Friend* is pushing it," she murmured.

Darcy looked at her. "Are you all right?"

"What exactly did you think I was going to do to her?" Quinn asked, more amused than offended.

Darcy finally put away his own SIG and closed the cabin door behind him. "What do you want?"

"I'm assuming the same thing you do. To find out who blew Rigsby's cover. Put them away and stop whatever they're planning."

"Why now?" McKenna asked.

Quinn waved toward the chair and sofa. "May I?"

Darcy shrugged and crossed to where McKenna stood, flattening his palm against the middle of her back. He led her to the sofa and sat closer, his thigh warm against her leg. "Talk."

Quinn sat in the armchair again, unhurriedly crossing his legs. "This morning, an FBI agent visited me at my apartment in town. Wanting to discuss my connection to Rigsby."

"What connection?" Darcy asked.

Quinn's sharp gaze met Darcy's. "Exactly."

"You mean, they're looking deep into my background," McKenna realized. "All the way to the beginning of my FBI career."

"That's my presumption."

McKenna felt Darcy's leg grow tense against hers.

"I assume if they connect you to me," Quinn continued, "they'll connect you to Darcy, as well."

"Are you suggesting we part company?" Darcy asked.

"Do you want to part company?"

"No," Darcy said firmly before McKenna could speak.

"Then no. But be aware that you may receive a visit from Agent Boyle."

Beside her, Darcy went utterly still. His thigh felt like a rock against hers. But otherwise, he showed no other sign of reaction.

Quinn looked at McKenna. "I assume you know Agent Boyle?"

"He's my supervisory special agent."

"Can he be trusted?"

Darcy's thigh pressed against hers for a moment, then relaxed.

"I don't really trust anyone at the FBI right now," she said. "But Boyle has always seemed to be a pretty straight arrow."

Quinn's scrutiny was almost uncomfortable. But his expression cleared, finally, and he rose. "I assume you'd like to be alone to discuss your options. You know how to reach me if you need my assistance."

"What makes you think you weren't followed here?" Darcy asked, rising to follow Quinn to the door.

Quinn gave him a pointed look as he opened the door and stepped out onto the porch.

"Call if you need anything." Quinn turned and left.

Darcy shut the door firmly behind Quinn and pressed his forehead against it. "We have to leave here again."

She sighed. "I know."

"I'm sorry."

"You're sorry?" She crossed to where he stood, impulsively sliding her arms around his waist from behind. She rested her cheek against his shoulder blade. "I honestly don't know what I'd have done if I hadn't come here, Darcy. You probably saved my life."

He turned, pulling her into the circle of his arms, his chin resting on her head for a moment. She felt utterly safe, she realized, despite the way danger seemed to be circling them, ever closer, seeking a chance to strike.

He let her go with a sigh. "We should pack. Quickly."

With a brief nod, she led the way to the bedroom to gather their things.

"So, THE ANONYMOUS unit commander was Darryl Boyle."

Darcy slanted a quick glance at McKenna. She sat straight and alert in the Land Rover's passenger seat, her gaze angled forward at the highway visible through the windshield. "You don't sound surprised."

"I got over the surprise back at the cabin when you telegraphed something was up with Boyle," she said drily. "You think there's any chance Quinn didn't notice your reaction?"

"No," he admitted. "Another set of eyes on Boyle won't hurt, will it?"

"Probably not," she admitted before falling silent.

They'd headed north when they left the cabin on Killshadow Road, bypassing the bigger tourist towns along the way in search of somewhere small and secluded to hide out for the next few days. Someone at the office had once told him about a motel in the Poe Creek area that took cash and didn't ask any questions.

Exactly the sort of place they needed.

They passed the highway sign announcing Poe Creek, Tennessee, was about fifteen miles ahead, before she spoke again. "Boyle has always struck me as a straight arrow. Law and order all the way. And—" She stopped short, pressing her lips to a thin line.

"And?"

"Well, I was about to say he's a fanatic about domestic terror investigations. Thinks we're ignoring the threat inside our own borders because we're too focused on foreign terror threats."

"He doesn't sound like a person likely to get in bed with the Blue Ridge Infantry."

"He doesn't," she agreed. "I find it hard to imagine he'd ever get involved with a group like the Blue Ridge Infantry. He's dedicated his life to bringing down groups just like them."

"But you're not certain about it, are you?"

She shook her head. "I've learned in this business, sometimes the perp is the last person you expect."

The Mountain Hideaway Motor Lodge in Poe Creek, Tennessee, was about what one would expect from a small, independent motor lodge on a main highway through the Appalachian Mountains. A rectangular two-story building constructed with now-fading red bricks and a flickering neon marquee in front of the office, the motel looked suitably shabby and anonymous for their purposes.

He parked the Land Rover in the side lot not easily visible from the street and turned to look at McKenna. "One room or two?"

Her gaze snapped up to meet his. "I'm really not sure how to answer that question."

He smiled at the wariness in her eyes. "For safety's sake. Do you feel safe in a room on your own or do you think we should band together so neither of us gets ambushed alone?"

Her lips quirked. "When you put it like that, one. I've been ambushed alone quite recently. It wasn't fun."

"Wait here. I'll pay for the room and get the key."

As promised, the clerk at the front desk of the motel office barely looked up from his paperback book to take Darcy's money and offer up a key. Darcy used his best American accent, in case the clerk was paying enough attention to remember later that his newest motel guest spoke with a British one, and signed in as Mr. and Mrs. Blake.

He found McKenna standing outside the Land Rover when he got back, stretching her legs. The afternoon breeze lifted her auburn curls and swirled them around her face. It was a good thing, he thought, that she'd stayed out here. Even the absentminded clerk couldn't have forgotten the sight of McKenna Rigsby and her glorious riot of hair.

"You should consider a ponytail," he told her as he unlocked the door to their first-floor room.

She gave him a side-eye glance as she preceded him into the room, reaching out to flick on the light switch as she passed. Dim light radiated weakly from the grimy overhead bulb. "Lovely."

"And a baseball cap."

She dropped the gym bag full of borrowed clothes they'd brought back with them from Hunter Bragg's cabin and looked at him, her head cocked to one side. "You don't like my hair?"

"I worship your hair," he answered with a smile. "But I'm not sure that it's good for the rest of the world to be quite so bedazzled by it if we're trying to keep a low profile."

Her smile felt like sunshine, warming the cool afternoon. "Duly noted."

The motel room was clean, at first glance. He'd stayed

in fleabag motels that hadn't put forth much effort at keeping up appearances, so he supposed it was to the Mountain Hideaway Motor Lodge's credit that he didn't automatically want to fumigate the entire room.

"I've stayed in worse," McKenna muttered as she set the gym bag on the bed nearest the bathroom and dropped to the edge of the mattress, her back to Darcy.

There was minimal furniture in the room—two full-size beds and a built-in dresser on the wall facing the beds. No chairs, no table, only two movable lamps by each bed, attached to the wall on a metal sconce. Darcy put down his duffel bag on the second bed and sat on the edge, as well, his gaze drawn to McKenna's slumped posture.

"Are you feeling well?" he asked finally when she didn't move.

She lifted her head and swiveled to look at him. "I have bullet holes in my side, I'm stuck in a cheap motel and I don't know who to trust. So, no. I'm not really feeling that well at the moment."

"Are you hungry? I could drive to one of those hamburger places we passed and get something for dinner."

"Maybe a salad."

He gave her a skeptical look, earning a hint of a smile from her.

"I know, veggies aren't my style, but I don't feel like eating anything heavy at the moment. Could go for a sweet tea, too."

He couldn't stop a grimace, but at least his show of distaste earned another smile from her. "I'll see if I can accommodate your culinary needs," he said in his most formal, clipped tone, determined to make that smile hang around a little longer.

"Knew I could count on you, Jeeves."

"Not a Brit," he murmured, getting up to leave.

Her grin followed him out the door.

He returned fifteen minutes later to the sight of McKenna sitting cross-legged on his bed, her fingers flying across the keyboard of his laptop. She looked up as he entered and set the bags of drive-through food on the dresser. "Hi."

"Hi." He was a little surprised she hadn't pulled her Glock on him. "I'm not sure you should drop your guard so easily."

"I saw you coming," she said with a cheeky smile. "Did you know you can tap into this fine establishment's security cameras by way of their free Wi-Fi?" She turned the computer around to show him the screen. Up in one corner was a small box showing a grainy black-and-white image of the breezeway in front of the external motel-room doors. "It's our own early-warning system."

"You know how to do that?"

The smile she flashed him sent tremors rolling through his chest to settle low in his belly. "Didn't the DSS teach you any computer tricks?"

"No, and why do I get the feeling you didn't learn that particular trick from the FBI, either?"

"Because I didn't," she admitted. "Remember that anarchist guy who had the hots for me?"

"Gecko?"

"Komodo," she corrected, slanting an amused look his way. "And it was Ax who had the hots for me. It was Komodo who thought he was dealing with a stupid hillbilly."

"Not a hillbilly?" he murmured.

"Not even close. I got Ax to show off all his tricks, pretending I didn't understand a thing about what he was doing. But, in fact, he was showing me how to do all kinds of things that are illegal as hell."

"Like tapping into a motel security camera?"

"Passive snooping. Barely illegal and nobody's likely

to find out in a place like this." She scooted over, making room for him on the bed.

He sat, trying not to touch her. But the soft mattress conspired against him, dipping with his weight and sending him arm to arm with her in the middle of the bed. "Any more tricks up your sleeve?"

When she slanted a look at him, her eyes were the deep green of the privet hedges that grew on the country estate where his mother preferred to spend most of the summers. "Lots."

His whole body seemed to flush hot, then cold, then hot again. This was worse than before, he thought. Back in Kaziristan, they'd kept a formal sort of distance from each other, physically, for the most part.

But now that he'd kissed her, doing so again—and doing so much more—seemed to be all he could think about.

He cleared his throat before he spoke. "Any more thoughts about Landry or Boyle? You've worked with both of them. You're in the best position between the two of us to know what we should do next."

"I honestly don't know. Right now, I'd say that Landry seems more likely, but that may be because I don't know him as well as Darryl Boyle. I've worked with Boyle almost a year now. Landry, I worked with for just a few weeks as part of a joint domestic terrorism investigation."

"But Ava Trent seems to concur with your assessment of Landry."

"What about Olivia Sharp? What did she say about Landry?"

"She seemed very cautious when speaking about Landry. There's something odd about her connection to him. I wish I'd had more time to delve deeper with her."

"How deep, exactly?"

The hint of jealousy he heard in McKenna's voice caught him by surprise. He let himself look at her again, bracing against the seismic effect she seemed to have on him recently.

Her wry smile told him she was mostly joking, but the curiosity in her eyes revealed he hadn't mistaken the slightly possessive tone of her voice.

"No more than skin deep."

"So she has nice skin?"

"Not nearly as nice as yours."

McKenna crinkled her nose. "I bet she's tall."

"Positively Amazonian."

"In ridiculously good shape," she ventured.

"Which indicates a rather unseemly obsession with one's appearance, wouldn't you say?"

"I would," she agreed, smiling so brightly he thought he could bask in her glow for the rest of his life. "I really would."

"She isn't you," he said softly. "No one else in the world is you."

"That's very cryptic."

He smiled. "Maybe you can get your friend Chainsaw to crack the code."

"Ax, Darcy. Ax." She set the laptop aside and shifted until she was on her knees beside him, gazing down at him with those fathomless green eyes. "I want this over with, Darcy. I want to be free again."

"I know. I want that for you."

"I've been thinking about how to do that. To get this over with faster."

He heard reluctance in her voice, as if she knew he wouldn't like what she was about to say. "What do you have in mind?" he asked.

"I think we should set a trap for both Landry and Boyle. I can contact each of them, tell them I want to come in from the cold and set a meeting time. Ask them to bring backup. Then we see which one of them brings backup and which one comes alone. The one who shows up alone isn't playing by the rules."

"What if they both bring backup? They'll take you in."

"At least we'll know neither of them is the mole in the FBI."

Darcy shook his head. "I don't want you putting yourself up as bait. Too much can go wrong."

"I'm tired of waiting around for us to stumble onto a break in this case. We need to make things happen or it's possible they never will."

As she made a move to get up off the bed, he caught her arm, stilling her movement. She gazed back at him, her eyes going dark. The air between them crackled with a sudden burst of heat, and even as he let go of her bare arm, he couldn't keep himself from letting his fingers trail down to the delicate skin of her slender wrist.

Her lips trembled apart. "Darcy—"

He tightened his grip on her wrist, tugging her to him until she stood between his legs, gazing down at him with a mixture of desire and consternation.

"Don't put yourself in danger, Rigsby." He wrapped his free arm around her waist, pulling her closer until her hips pressed against his belly.

"Are you going to try to seduce me out of it?" Her voice was warm velvet.

"Will it work?" he asked, pressing his mouth against the collarbone peeking out of her T-shirt collar.

"Worth a try," she said as she pushed him back onto the bed.

Chapter Fourteen

She felt reckless. Impulsive. Completely out of control. All the things she'd struggled with her whole life, that wild hare scampering inside her soul, yearning for wide-open spaces and spectacular adventures.

Her mother had warned her early about letting her feral side take control. Wild hares got eaten by predators. Run over by cars. They lived short, adrenaline-fueled lives. They never won the race.

But oh, the feel of flying along at breakneck speed, your heart galloping in your breast like a Thoroughbred going for the win—it was an intoxicating sensation. Darcy's arms around her were strong and solid, holding her so tightly as he kissed her that she thought she might break.

But she was stronger than his passion. Stronger than her own fierce response. She twined her fingers with his and kissed him deeply, with abandon, needing this freedom, this moment of surrender and demand.

But she couldn't let herself lose all control. She couldn't. Walking away from her friendship with Darcy had been one of the hardest things she'd ever done.

How much harder would it be to leave him behind if they gave in to this wicked fire burning between them?

Darcy dragged his mouth away from her jaw and looked up at her. "What's wrong?"

"This thing between us here—it can't go anywhere, can it?"

His chest rose and fell beneath her. "You are possibly the most confounding woman I've ever known."

He dropped his hands and she rolled away, lying on her back beside him. She stared up at the cheap light fixture overhead and wished her mother's voice had stayed silent a few minutes longer.

"I'm sorry," she murmured.

"I don't know if what's going on between us here can go anywhere. My life at the moment is nothing but a question mark. And you're wanted by the FBI." He reached across the narrow space between them and took her hand. "I just know that when I made it stateside after the siege, I felt utterly gutted because you weren't there. And I also know what we were about to do here was reckless and ill-advised."

"I'm sorry." She turned her head, taking in his handsome profile, the way his brow furrowed as he gazed up at the ceiling. "I know you think I'm a rule-breaking wild card compared to you, but I'm not the incautious type, really. I just—I missed you, Darcy. Every damn day."

He turned his head, his dark eyes meeting hers. "I missed you, too. You were an island of sanity in Kaziristan. Bloody levelheaded hillbilly. Nothing fazed you."

"Not a hillbilly."

"Yes, you are." He turned his body toward hers, reaching out to touch her face. "In the very best sense of the word. You're as solid as the mountains. As brave as the settlers who built a life on this rocky soil. As practical and unsentimental as any hardy mountaineer who's ever roamed these hills. I depended on every bit of that strength, McKenna, all those years ago in Kaziristan. I'm depending on it now."

His words brought tears to her eyes. She blinked them back. "So much for unsentimental."

He smiled and leaned forward to press his lips against her forehead. "I know you want this over with. But the thought of putting you out there like a piece of bear bait—"

"We can set it up so that it's safe." At his skeptical look, she added, "Or as safe as we can make it."

"If you insist on doing this, we need to bring Quinn in on the plan."

She shook her head, remembering Quinn's earlier visit to the cabin. "He's working his own agenda, Darcy. You know he is. It's what he does."

"Yes, but it so happens that his agenda coincides with ours."

"Until it doesn't." She sat up, letting go of his hand. "And there's the problem of the mole in your agency, too. I know it's not you. But there's someone leaking information from there, right?"

"Yes."

"Who else is under suspicion?"

"A man named Anson Daughtry. He, Quinn and I were the only three people who knew the real identity of an undercover operative working for The Gates. Someone got wind of that information, as well as what she was doing. She was lucky to survive. But she had to leave Tennessee."

"Is she in WitSec?" McKenna asked, her stomach aching. She'd dealt with a handful of people over the years who ended up in Witness Security, their names, their whole identities erased and replaced with new lives. Not all of them were innocent victims, of course, but there had been a few whose lives were shattered entirely through no fault of their own.

"No. And I don't know where she is now, because I could be the mole." His voice was tight with anger. "I need this to be over, but I don't know how to defend myself. All I have is my good name, my reputation, and that means nothing to Quinn."

"I think it means something," she disagreed, reaching for his hand and twining her fingers through his. "Quinn knows you're innocent. I could tell by the way he spoke to you. He respects you, and he doesn't respect traitors."

"Then why am I still on leave?"

"I think maybe because you're serving his purposes where you are. Such as your propensity for taking in wayward FBI agents in need."

He squeezed her fingers. "I'm a complete sucker for a wayward FBI agent in need."

"He trusts you." She looked down at their entwined hands. "The problem is, I don't trust him. Right now, I don't trust anyone but you."

He brought her hand to his lips and kissed her knuckles. "You know that question you asked me earlier? About whether I thought things between us could go anywhere?"

She nodded, not sure she wanted to hear the answer.

"I want it to. I do." He grasped her hand between his, holding it to his chest. "I have spent a very long time believing I would always be alone in life. And the thought never bothered me that much. I was an only child, raised by parents who loved me but never really enjoyed my company. They had their own lives to live, and they believed that coddling me too much would do me more harm than good."

Her heart contracted at the picture he was painting of his childhood. Her own had been nearly the opposite, she thought, a life spent under the watchful but loving eye of a mother who had made McKenna her whole world. "That must have been a lonely life."

He shook his head. "It didn't feel that lonely, really. The staff was kind. And my father's sister enjoyed my company a great deal when she visited. But she was so far away in America." He smiled. "It's one of the reasons I went to college in America instead of at Oxford as my father had hoped. Aunt Vivian was a graduate of the University of Virginia, and she talked me into going there."

"Sounds like you enjoyed it."

"Immensely." His smile faded. "But Aunt Viv died my senior year at UVA. Car accident. All very sudden."

"I'm sorry."

"So, I became accustomed to my own company." He slanted a look at her. "Until I went to Kaziristan to protect the ambassador and stumbled upon a wild-haired water nymph in the embassy pool."

She laughed. "Now you're just making things up. Water nymph?"

"Flitting through the water, all hair and fair skin and big green eyes. I was mesmerized."

"Darcy, you ordered me out of the pool."

"That's not the way I remember it."

"You told me I didn't have authorization to be there."

"I did no such thing."

"You were imperious and aggravating. You sounded like a snotty butler in a bad British movie."

He smiled more broadly. "Not a Brit."

"Yes, you are. The very best kind of Brit—smart, capable, steeped in traditions worth keeping and endowed with a dry wit that kept me sane in the middle of hell."

He cleared his throat. "Well, then. It seems we're both paragons."

She laughed. "We are. We really are."

His lips curled in a smile that didn't make it all the way to his eyes. "I know you want this to be over. I do, too. But if we just throw you out there to the wolves without a plan—"

"Who says we aren't going to have a plan?"

DARCY'S BURGER HAD gone cold by the time he pulled out their dinner from the take-out bags, but he ate it anyway, listening to McKenna work her way through their options between bites of her partially wilted salad.

"We're looking for somewhere that has public Wi-Fi and a decent video-surveillance system," she said after washing down a bite of salad with the sweet tea she'd ordered. "The more angles of approach we can cover the better. And we need to get our hands on another laptop computer so that we can cover both places we set up as the rendezvous points."

"I have a credit card, but if people are looking for me now—"

"You wanted to bring Quinn in on this plan, right?"

"But you said—"

"I don't trust him with the details. But if he can arrange for you to get your hands on a computer, I won't object."

Darcy set his burger on the bedside table and grabbed his duffel bag. He'd purchased a disposable phone shortly after going on administrative leave, aware that in his line of business, stealth might become a necessity before his ordeal was over.

Especially if someone in The Gates was setting both him and Anson Daughtry up for a fall.

He turned on the phone and checked the battery. Still had over 60 percent power. He'd need to charge it soon. But it would do what he needed for now.

He dialed a number only a handful of people knew. Even most of the agents at The Gates didn't have Quinn's personal number.

Quinn answered on the second ring. "Bradford Building Supply," he answered in a broad mountain drawl that made Darcy smile.

"It's your wayward son," Darcy replied.

"Is something wrong?" Quinn dropped the accent.

"I need a laptop computer. Performance oriented, with wireless and the means to monitor a video feed."

"Don't ask for a lot, do you?"

"Can you supply it?" Darcy asked, trying to keep his impatience from bleeding into his voice.

He could tell by the tone of Quinn's voice that he hadn't been entirely successful. "Would you like to tell me why I should?"

"Because you asked me to protect someone and I'm doing my best to accomplish that task. But I need a computer."

"What are you two up to?"

"Do you trust me to do this job or not?"

"Technically—"

"I'm on administrative leave. I know that. Believe me." Darcy glanced across the motel room at the other bed, where McKenna was conducting a web search for potential sites where they could set up rendezvous points with access to security-video feeds. "But you know as well as I do that you've given me a job to do. Do you trust me to do it or don't you?"

"I don't give jobs to people I don't trust."

Darcy felt the bunched muscles in his shoulders relax. "How quickly can you have the laptop ready for me?"

"Do you have twenty-four hours?"

"If need be."

"I'll try to make it faster. I don't have your phone number—"

"I know," Darcy said and hung up.

McKenna glanced up at him. "You're actually very sexy when you're being imperious and aggravating."

He smiled. "How's the search coming?"

"I have a list of six potential places. We'll have to check them out to make sure I can tap into the feeds. Some places may have heavier encryption than this motel. Some places won't. How long before Quinn can deliver a second laptop?"

"Twenty-four hours."

She nodded. "That will give us time. I think we should

try to get some sleep this afternoon and plan to go site hunting late in the evening. These sites I've picked out probably aren't going to shut down their Wi-Fi connections at night. If they do, they're probably heavily encrypted anyway and of little use to us."

He crossed to her side, looking over her shoulder at the list. There were two fast-food restaurants, a handful of motels, hotels or lodges, a campground and a coffee shop, all in or around the Poe Creek area. "The campground may be too remote. And I'm not sure what kind of security cameras they'd have available to tap into."

"We'll find out when we drive there tonight," she said with a shrug, handing over the laptop. "You figure out a plan of attack. I need a nap." She stretched out on her back, closing her eyes.

"We haven't treated your wounds since after your shower last night," he said. "I know you're feeling better, but we can't assume they're all healed up."

With a groan, she turned onto her side, lifting up the edge of her T-shirt. "Go for it, Marquis de Sade."

Forcing his gaze away from the curve of her slender waist, he grabbed the first-aid kit from his duffel bag and gathered his supplies. They were getting low on several, including gauze and other bandaging materials. "You didn't notice a drugstore near any of those places we need to go tonight, did you?"

"I think there's one not far from the burger place on Greenbrier Road." She looked at him over her shoulder. "How are we standing on money?"

"Good for now." He'd withdrawn five thousand dollars on his last trip to Purgatory, so with a little judicious budgeting, they wouldn't run out of cash anytime soon.

He eased the bandage away from her wounds, wincing a little as the tape pulled at her skin. She sucked in a quick breath but had no other reaction.

The wounds were healing. The redness of infection was all but gone, only the ragged edges of the wounds themselves still red with inflammation. And even they were starting to close up and scab over.

"How's it look?" she asked.

"Hideous," he said lightly. "But we've fought back the infection."

"Hideous, huh?" She shot him a wry grin. "You always know how to make me feel pretty."

Smiling back, he used a couple of his dwindling supply of antiseptic wipes to clean up the wounds. "Your wounds are dry and healing. You want to try going without a bandage awhile?"

She shot him an eager look. "I would love that. The tape pulls and itches like hell."

He tugged her T-shirt hem down to cover the wounds, his hands remarkably steady given how hard his heart was pounding. Even doing something as mundane and unsexy as cleaning her wounds was enough to get his pulse racing and his skin prickling.

He was so much more vulnerable to her now than he ever remembered being. Was it the proximity? The constant threat of discovery?

Or was it the fact that he'd finally allowed himself to touch her, to kiss her and hold her the way he'd wanted to that very first night at the embassy in Tablis? One taste and he was a helpless addict?

"Darcy?"

He made himself look at her. She was gazing back at him with a quizzical look on her face. "What?" he asked, his voice coming out low and hoarse.

"Is something wrong?" She touched his hand, the mere brush of her fingers sparking his nerves until they jangled.

He moved away from her, needing the distance. "Everything's fine."

He heard the mattress creak, then her footsteps as she walked up behind him. He looked up at the dresser mirror and saw her standing behind him, her gaze soft and worried.

"Darcy—"

He closed his eyes. "I should take the Land Rover down the road and fill up the gas tank if we're going to be driving around all evening."

Her hand closed over his shoulder, her grip gentle. "Are you running away, Darcy?"

He opened his eyes and met her knowing gaze. He couldn't quite stop a wry smile from quirking his lips. "Yes," he admitted.

She dropped her hand away and smiled back. "Go ahead. Just don't go far. I was serious about trying to get some sleep before we go back out tonight. I don't think we should try to get started before ten. We don't need a lot of people out and about, wondering what we're up to."

He left quickly, pausing beside the driver's door of the Land Rover for a moment, breathing in the chilled spring air. Clouds gathered in the west, promising rain.

It might turn out to be a miserable sort of night, he thought, wondering if they should postpone their hunting expedition for another night.

But what was the alternative—spending all night in bed across from McKenna, wanting her but not letting himself have her?

He pulled out his burner phone as he slid behind the wheel of the Land Rover and dialed Cain Dennison's number.

"HE'S UP TO SOMETHING," Olivia said from her perch on the edge of Quinn's desk. She didn't even bother with the niceties anymore, Quinn thought, watching her fiddle with the pencil holder in front of his desk blotter. "He was asking all sorts of questions about the Richmond incident."

"I suppose he suspects Cade Landry of blowing McKenna Rigsby's cover with the BRI," Quinn said, keeping an eye on Olivia's face.

Her expression didn't shift, but there was a flicker of something in her blue eyes. "Probably. He was also asking about another agent, Darryl Boyle. Last I heard, Boyle was an SSA in the Knoxville Field Office."

So, Quinn thought. They had two suspects. And Darcy wanted to get his hands on a second laptop computer, with wireless and reliable video-streaming capability.

Just what the hell was Darcy up to?

McKenna hadn't expected to fall asleep while Darcy was out, but apparently her stamina hadn't returned as much as she'd thought, for when she next opened her eyes, darkness had fallen outside the motel room, only the muddy light of the parking-lot lamps relieving the gloom.

She sat up, blinking away sleep, and reached for the bedside lamp to check her watch. Almost nine.

Then she realized Darcy's bed was empty.

"Darcy?" She got up and went into the bathroom.

Empty.

"Darcy?" She went back out to the main area and looked around thoroughly, though there was nowhere in the tiny room for anyone to hide, especially a man as big and solid as Darcy. She even ventured outside the motel room to check the back parking lot for any sign of the Land Rover.

It wasn't there.

She hurried to the room and closed herself inside, her heart hammering in her chest.

How long had he been gone? At least three hours, right? He had left around six, just as night was beginning to fall.

"Oh, Darcy," she whispered to the empty motel room as she sank onto the end of his bed. "Where the hell are you?"

Chapter Fifteen

Headlights appeared in the gloom, coming around a blind curve in the twisting mountain road where Darcy had parked the Land Rover. He was outside the vehicle, hidden, unwilling to make quite so easy a target in case Cain Dennison had double-crossed him.

The headlights dimmed and extinguished, and as Darcy's eyes adjusted to the gloom, he could make out the massive cab of Dennison's F-150 in the pale wash of moonlight. The driver's door opened, engaging the dome light inside the truck cab. Dennison hadn't come alone as asked, Darcy saw with a grimace. The girlfriend had tagged along.

The deputy-sheriff girlfriend.

Sara Lindsey's dark eyes scanned the scene, ever the cop, looking for signs of trouble in even the most mundane of situations. And Darcy supposed meeting a suspended agent up to his neck in skulduggery was hardly a mundane situation.

He stepped out of the shadows as they approached the Land Rover. "So much for coming alone."

Both Dennison and his girlfriend jerked their heads toward him in unison. "You try telling her no," Dennison drawled.

Darcy looked at Sara, who met his gaze steadily. "This is not a police matter."

Her lips curved, just a hint. "You're not a cop, so I'm not

sure you get to make that decision. But, for the record, I'm not here as a sheriff's deputy. And I know sometimes the letter of the law gets in the way of justice. I'm here to help."

"I've heard that before," Darcy murmured. He looked at Dennison. "Tell me why I should trust you after this."

"Because I'm all you've got," Dennison retorted. "I get that you don't do the friend thing. I've never been that great at it myself. But I know you're an honorable man. I know you're not the mole."

"You certainly should," Darcy said bluntly. "You've spent the last few weeks pretending to be my friend in order to investigate me."

"I wanted to clear you."

Darcy shook his head. "This was a bad idea. Forget I called." He started toward the Land Rover.

Sara caught his arm, her grip strong, stilling his movement. He looked down at her, irritated but also a little intrigued. Most of what he knew about Dennison's girlfriend had come from her part in a case Dennison had been investigating for The Gates, a twenty-year-old cold case involving Sara's deceased sister-in-law. Darcy's knowledge of that particular case was limited to what he'd heard around the office, but the subsequent news reports after the killer was captured had been enough to convince Darcy that Dennison's new girl was a hell of a lot tougher than she looked. And she looked plenty tough.

"Cain says you're in trouble. Let us help."

"I'm not in trouble," Darcy denied.

"But McKenna Rigsby is."

Darcy tried not to react to Dennison's soft reply. But when he looked up at his fellow agent, outlined in moon glow, understanding gleamed in Dennison's eyes.

"The FBI is trying to find you for questioning in her disappearance. They did a check of all the homes and businesses located on or around Killshadow Road, where the missing agent was last seen. Your name showed up, and a background check revealed your connection to her. You were both working at the US Embassy in Kaziristan eight years ago."

"So?"

"She's with you, isn't she?" Sara asked.

He looked at her, not answering.

"The FBI thinks she's gone rogue," Dennison said. "Ignored an order to come in from an undercover assignment. She fired shots at some hunters in the woods, unprovoked—"

Darcy arched an eyebrow at Dennison.

"I am aware that the hunters were probably militia members," Dennison added quietly. "And that she's the one being hunted."

Darcy looked away.

"Quinn knows something is up, but he's not talking. Not to me, anyway." Dennison shrugged. "I can't help if I don't know what's going on."

"I need someone to provide backup," Darcy said.

"Backup for what?"

"I'm trying to flush someone into the open."

"The real rogue in the FBI?" Sara asked.

Darcy didn't answer. He supposed Dennison and his girlfriend would find his silence answer enough.

"What do you need?" Dennison asked finally. "How much backup?"

"I need at least six people who can handle themselves in a fight."

"Do you plan to tell them more about what's going on than you've told us?" Sara's voice was tinged with doubt.

"I don't know," Darcy admitted. "I have to figure out all of the logistics."

"She doesn't know you're talking to us, does she?" Sara asked.

"No."

She closed her eyes and shook her head.

"I think I can rustle up six people who'll help you without asking a lot of questions." Dennison sighed. "That's the easy part."

"What's the hard part?" Darcy asked.

"You get to tell Agent Rigsby you arranged for backup without informing her." Sara turned and started walking toward the truck.

"Good luck." Dennison clapped Darcy on the back and followed Sara to the truck.

Darcy watched them leave before he climbed into the Land Rover and settled behind the steering wheel. Dennison and his girlfriend were right. He should have told McKenna what he was going to do.

Except he knew she wouldn't have agreed. Her current supply of trust was severely limited. There was no way she'd have agreed to bringing strangers into their plans. And now her trust in him was going to take one hell of a hit when he confessed what he'd done.

He still wouldn't change it. He'd done what he'd had to do.

But at what cost?

THE HOUR HAND of her watch clicked over. Ten o'clock. And still no Darcy. At first she'd been worried. Then angry.

Now she was worried again.

She'd tried to go back to sleep, reasoning that she could use the rest, and sleep would make time pass more quickly. But her nerves were too frayed for her to relax, and every time she closed her eyes in the dark motel room, a dozen different scenarios played out in her mind, dangers that she knew all too well were more than just her imagination at work.

There were people out there who wanted her dead. And if they'd connected Darcy to her the way Quinn said they had—

Car beams flashed through the motel-room curtains, painting arcs of light across the walls before the darkness swallowed the room again. She heard the growl of an engine die away in the night, followed a couple of minutes later by the sound of footsteps walking down the breezeway outside the room.

She sat up quickly, reaching for her Glock. It might be Darcy coming back. But considering how long he'd been gone, it could easily be someone else altogether.

There was a rattle of the doorknob. The swish of a card in the door lock. The door opened a few inches and Darcy's voice came through the narrow space. "Rigsby, it's me. I'm alone."

She didn't lower the pistol. But her heart leaped at the sound of his voice.

He entered slowly, sliding through the narrow doorway and shutting the door behind him. Only then did he flick the switch, turning on the overhead light.

McKenna checked him over quickly with her gaze, cataloging intact sets of limbs, the correct number of fingers, no signs of blood or injury. Relief set in, quickly eclipsed by anger, and she put the Glock down and crossed the room in four angry strides. "Where the hell have you been?"

"You know I went to get gas in the Land Rover."

"Hours ago."

"Large tank," he said, his tone infuriatingly dry.

"That's not funny." She thumped his chest with her hand.

He trapped her hand in place. "I didn't know the phone number for this room or I'd have called. I should have written it down."

"You could have called the front desk and had them patch you through." She wanted to stay furious at him, but his thumb was doing things to the back of her hand that made her want to curl up like a kitten and purr.

"We're trying to maintain a low profile," he reminded

her, his head dipping until she could feel his breath against her cheek. "I'm sorry."

"Where were you?" She tried to sound demanding, but her question came out on a plaintive sigh.

"Let's sit down." He led her to the bed and sat her down, crouching in front of her.

She didn't like the serious, troubled look in his dark eyes. "Has something happened?"

"Not yet," he answered, taking both of her hands in his. "But something's going to happen as soon as we figure out our plan of action."

"What's that?" She sounded breathless, even to her own ears.

"We're going to have backup."

A cold sensation swamped her with shocking suddenness. A soft buzzing sound rang in her ears. "We're going to have what?"

"I met with Cain Dennison. I told him we need backup for our plan."

She had to be dreaming still. It would explain the sudden, shivery feeling of unreality assaulting her with a vengeance, turning her limbs to liquid and making her heart thump with dread. "No. You wouldn't do that. You wouldn't go behind my back and set me up that way."

"I didn't set you up—"

She pulled her hands away from his, her fingers tingling. "Darcy, I told you no. I told you I wanted to handle this my way. Without bringing other people into it. My God, you told Dennison I was with you?"

Darcy pushed to his feet, sliding his hands through his crisp, dark hair. "He already knew. He's not stupid. The FBI has already connected you to me—you think Dennison didn't connect us, too? He saw me at Bragg's cabin. He knows I wasn't playing caretaker for Bragg—one phone call to your cousin's fiancé would have blown that story to pieces."

"That's not the same thing as you seeking him out behind my back and confirming it to him." She couldn't sit still, her legs suddenly jittering with nervous energy. "Darcy, your company has a mole working inside it. It's not you, but for all you know, it could be any other person who works there."

"At least you don't think it's me," he murmured, his gaze following her as she paced back and forth beside him. "Small favors."

She stopped in front of him. "Do you think that's funny?"

"I think we're outgunned, outnumbered and, if we don't improve our chances against the people gunning for you, we'll be outsmarted, as well."

"It's not your decision to make!"

"If I'm putting my life on the line for you, it damned well is!"

"Not without consulting me!"

"Would you have agreed to it?"

"No."

"Then what was the point of consulting you?"

She stared at him. He did not just say that. "I beg your pardon?"

"I don't think we can do this without backup. It would be foolhardy. Insane. Even if the plan works—even if you flush out the FBI's turncoat—what guarantee do we have that he's come alone? If he's in bed with the Blue Ridge Infantry, isn't it far more likely that he'd bring a crew with him to make sure his mess gets mopped up thoroughly?"

"We'll have advance notice."

"So we'll see our deaths coming."

"Damn it, Darcy!" She felt gutted, she realized. Upended, as if he'd jerked the floor from beneath her feet and sent her into free fall.

She sank to the edge of the bed, feeling sick.

"I know you're angry at me," he said quietly, reaching for her hand.

She jerked it away. "Don't try to handle me."

He dropped his hands to his sides.

"You had no right to do this without talking to me," she growled, trying hard not to let the tears beating at the backs of her eyes spill over. "Do you realize the danger you've put me in?"

"You were already in danger. I'm trying to get you free of it."

She made herself look at him, even though the sight of him right now made her want to punch him right in that beautiful mouth. "I came to you for help because I didn't have anywhere else to go. I should have remembered what you're like."

His eyes narrowed. "What I'm like?"

"Protocol says to procure backup, so that's what you do." Her voice was flint-hard. Good. She felt like stone inside. "You never even stopped to consider I might have my own ideas about how to protect myself, did you? Of course you didn't. You're the big bad security consultant. The man. Right?"

"This is not a man-woman issue."

"You're very right about that," she said coolly. "There's no man-woman anything about you and me. Not now."

His eyes closed for a moment. "McKenna."

"I think we function better when you remember that I'm Special Agent Rigsby with the FBI. Under suspicion or not, I do know what I'm doing. I don't need some civilian rent-a-cop telling me how to do my job."

His eyes snapped open, blazing back at her. "That was beneath you, Agent Rigsby."

"Do you think I haven't considered the idea that we could use backup? I have. The FBI may have painted me as a rogue agent, but I'm not one. I do know the protocols and the reasons they exist. I just can't depend on them under these circumstances. I don't know whom to trust." She leveled her gaze with his, making sure he was looking at her. "Maybe I would have been better off trusting no one at all."

"I don't deserve that." His voice was low and tight.

"Maybe you don't," she conceded. "But I can't take any chances."

He stepped backward, settling with his hips against the edge of the dresser, and fell silent.

She was tempted to walk out of the motel room and leave him behind for good. But she'd just made a big deal about not being stupid. It would hardly bolster her case to do something so monumentally dumb.

"I can call it off," he said a few minutes of silence later.

"It's too late."

"I trust Dennison," he added.

"But I don't even know him."

"You know me." Darcy pushed away from the dresser and crouched in front of her again, closing his hands over her elbows, holding her in place as he pinned her with his gaze. "You know me, Rigsby. You do. I'm the same man I've always been. And if there's anything in this world you should know about me, it's that I would never let anyone or anything hurt you if it's within my power. You have to know that about me."

She did know it. She might be angry now, might feel overturned and out of control, but she knew Darcy would put his life on the line for her, just as she would for him.

They'd always been bullet catchers, she and Darcy.

"I do know," she admitted.

"Then trust me. If I know anything at all about Cain Dennison, it's that he's a decent man. A good man. And he knows what's at stake. He will be as careful as you or I would be."

She couldn't be as certain as he was. She didn't know Cain Dennison. She didn't know how careful he would be or even if he knew what was at stake. And maybe if he was the only person she had to take a chance on trusting, she could do it for Darcy's sake.

"He's going to be approaching other people for you, isn't he?"

Darcy nodded.

"Do you know whom he'll be talking to?"

"No," Darcy admitted.

She rubbed her forehead, feeling the start of a headache between her eyes. "Every extra person who gets involved in this situation is another chance for betrayal."

Darcy released a long, slow breath. "Do you want me to contact Dennison and tell him to call it off?"

"Yes," she answered without thinking.

But as he reached into his pocket for his phone, she caught his arm, stilling his movement. He gave her a quizzical look.

"Just ask him to stand by. We need time before he contacts anyone else." She let go of him. "I need time."

With a nod, he pulled out his phone and made the call.

As he spoke in low tones with Cain Dennison, she pulled Darcy's notebook computer into her lap. She'd made a list of places to check out tonight, and it was past time for them to get started.

She'd worry about the question of backup later. Right now, they had to find out if there was any hope of their plan working at all.

By two in the morning, Darcy was beginning to wish he'd stuck around the motel room that afternoon and grabbed a nap. Between his lack of sleep and the monotonous hum of the Land Rover's tires on the road top, their circuitous tour of Ridge County's hinterlands was lulling him dangerously close to falling asleep at the wheel.

In the passenger seat, McKenna seemed to have found her second wind, though he could only infer her state of mind because she'd spoken very little since they climbed into the Land Rover almost three hours earlier.

"So we're agreed on the two venues?" he asked finally. His voice seemed loud in the silence inside the SUV.

"The Econo-Tel and the Blackberry Café," she answered briskly, as if she didn't want her words to linger long enough to permanently break the chilly silence between them.

The Econo-Tel was a small, low-budget motor lodge on Pike Road just south of Poe Creek. Set back from the road in an otherwise rural area, it was just isolated enough to pose a temptation to someone who wanted to catch McKenna out in the middle of nowhere, far enough from civilization to make running for help difficult at best.

The Blackberry Café in the tiny mountain town of Brightwater was a little less secluded, flanked on the left by a hardware store and on the right by a television-repair shop. But if they set up the rendezvous after five in the evening, both of those shops would be closed for the night, only the diner still open.

The bigger question was, would either Boyle or Landry show up if McKenna reached out to them? And what if both of them followed protocol and brought an FBI team with them to the meeting?

As he pulled to a stop at a crossroads, McKenna turned suddenly toward him, her eyes glittering darkly in the faint glow of his dashboard lights. "We need backup," she said flatly. "You were right."

He stared at her, not sure he'd understood her. "I'm sorry. Did you just say I was right?"

The corners of her lips twitched, but she didn't smile. "I'm still really angry at you for contacting your friend without consulting me. You had no right, and it shows a distinct arrogance I don't like at all. But if we're going to lure in a mole in the FBI, we need to be better prepared than two people can be all alone. So do it. Call Dennison and tell him it's a go."

Darcy pulled out his phone, pausing with his hand over the number pad. "And what if you're right and I'm wrong?"

She leaned her head against the headrest. "Then God help us all."

Chapter Sixteen

Smoky Joe's Tavern in Bitterwood, Tennessee, was doing a brisk business for a Thursday night. McKenna followed Darcy into the bar to a table in the back near the pool table, still feeling a little fuzzy-headed from a day spent trying to catch up with sleep before they put their plan into action that night.

Darcy held out her chair for her before taking a seat across from her, his gaze cutting toward a couple circling the felt-topped pool table. The man—tall, broad-shouldered, thirty-something—bent to speak in the woman's ear. The woman nodded and crossed to the bar to place an order, while the man set his cue stick against the wall and settled at a table next to Darcy and McKenna.

"You're late," the man murmured, his voice barely audible over the din of the bar.

"Didn't want to appear overeager," Darcy replied in the same conversational tone. "Rigsby, this is Sutton Calhoun. The woman who was trouncing him at billiards is his wife, Ivy. She's a detective on the Bitterwood police force."

McKenna let her gaze drift toward the woman standing at the bar, talking to a burly man with thinning brown hair and a bushy beard. Ivy Calhoun was small and slim, with dark hair pulled back in a ponytail under a faded blue baseball cap. She glanced back at the table where her husband sat, letting her gaze slide unhurriedly over Darcy and McKenna before she turned back to accept a couple of longneck beers from the bartender.

With the same nonchalance that had characterized her glance their way, she sat across from her husband, handing him one of the beer bottles.

Sutton took a sip of the beer before speaking. "Ivy, you know Darcy."

Ivy nodded, not looking at them. "I do. I suppose you're going to give me some code name for his lady friend, even though we all know exactly who she is, right?" She spoke with a drawl that was pure Appalachia, tinted by a mild exasperation that told McKenna just what she thought of the cloak-and-dagger aspect of the night's agenda.

"Call me Mac," McKenna murmured.

"Whatever." Ivy took a sip of beer. "Y'all ready?"

"We're going somewhere?" Darcy asked.

"Been a little change of plans," Sutton murmured, setting the bottle of beer on the table in front of him. He ran his finger over the lip of the bottle. "Dennison thinks we're too exposed here."

"I don't like sudden changes of plan," McKenna muttered to Darcy. "How do we know this isn't a setup?"

"Because my husband and I don't do setups," Ivy answered.

"Says the woman I've never met before in my life."

Ivy made a low snorting sound and took another sip of beer.

"I know them," Darcy said quietly. "And I know Dennison. If he thinks this place is too exposed, he has a reason."

God, she hated this. Hated being at the mercy of anyone, needing their help so much that she was actually sitting here considering the idea of following two complete strangers God knew where to meet more strangers she was supposed to trust, sight unseen, to help her stay out of the hands of people who wanted her dead.

Darcy reached across the table and covered her hand with his, his gaze intent. "Do you trust me?"

She closed her eyes and took a leap of faith. "Yes."

"You leave first," Sutton said. "There's a small clearing just across the bridge on the right. People use it to turn around all the time. Pull into that turnabout and wait for us. We'll head out of here in five minutes. We're in a blue Silverado. When we pass, follow."

As a buxom brunette waitress started to approach, Darcy waylaid her with a smile. "My wife has a headache. I think we're just going to pack it in for now." He pulled out his wallet and handed her a five-dollar bill. "For your trouble." He reached for McKenna's hand, his gaze locking with hers once more.

She took his hand and let him lead her back out to the parking lot. "I don't like this."

"Can't say I'm happy about it myself," he admitted as he unlocked the Land Rover's passenger door to let her in. "But if Dennison believes we could be compromised by staying here, I'm going to hear him out."

Darcy pulled off the road in the shallow turnoff Sutton Calhoun had mentioned, putting the car in Park and leaving the engine to idle. He turned to look at her, not speaking.

Waiting, she realized, for her to speak.

"I'm afraid." It wasn't what she'd planned to say, but it rang with the sound of truth.

"As am I," he admitted. "But you're right that we have to do something to draw your enemies into the open."

A moment later, a Chevrolet Silverado drove slowly past. Darcy put the Land Rover in gear and followed.

Old Purgatory Road wound south through Bitterwood, then changed names to Smoky Crest Road as it curved east into the mountains just outside the national park. "Where are we now?" McKenna asked as the Land Rover slowed into a sharp switchback.

"Smoky Ridge," Darcy answered, his brow furrowed.

"Is that good or bad?"

"It's neither at the moment," he said calmly. But the furrows in his brow deepened the higher they climbed up the mountain road.

Ahead, the Silverado turned off the main road onto a side road. It was paved, which was the best thing that could be said for the narrow, rutted avenue that cut a curvy path through deepening woods.

It ended near the top of the rise at a small, rustic-looking cabin set in the middle of a tiny clearing. A concrete patio about eight feet square led to two concrete steps up to a screen door. Lights were on inside the cabin, but the curtains were closed and there was no obvious sign of movement inside.

Anxiety crept up her back. "Where is this?"

"It's a cabin," Darcy said unhelpfully.

"Whose?"

"I'm not certain."

Sutton and his dark-haired wife exited the Silverado, not waiting for Darcy and McKenna to follow them inside.

Darcy looked at McKenna. "Your call."

"We're here already," she said after a brief hesitation. "Let's see what's going on."

On the walk to the cabin door, McKenna saw what the glare of the headlights had hidden—two more trucks parked off the road, hidden by the shadows of the sheltering trees. "Do you recognize the vehicles?" she asked Darcy as his gaze slanted toward the trucks.

"One is Dennison's. He probably has Sara with him."

"And the other?"

"I think it's Mark Fitzpatrick's truck. He just traded his

old one in for a newer model shortly before I went on suspension, but I'm pretty sure that's the new truck."

As they reached the patio, the door opened and a tall, lean man stepped into the opening. "I'm Cain Dennison. I hear we're supposed to call you Mac. Come on in. Everybody's waiting to hear what you want us to do."

With a glance at Darcy, McKenna climbed the shallow steps and entered the cabin.

Inside, Cain Dennison went to stand next to a dark-haired woman she assumed must be his cop girlfriend. Nearby, the Calhouns were pouring themselves cups of coffee at the counter. Two other men filled out the group gathered around the small kitchen table—a tall, attractive man with short brown hair and intelligent hazel-green eyes and a second man whose dark, spiky hair and vulpine features reminded her of a feral animal, all nerves and sinew. His mobile mouth curved in a smile as she met his gaze, but she wasn't sure she entirely trusted its sincerity.

"Mac," Ivy Calhoun said, with a slight arch of her dark eyebrows indicating she was annoyed at having to pretend she didn't know McKenna's real name, "you met Cain at the door. That's his fiancée, Sara."

Darcy's gaze snapped up. "Fiancée?"

Cain's smile lit up his face. "She said yes."

"Congratulations."

"You're a cop," McKenna murmured to Sara as the woman reached out to shake hands.

Sara's smile was tight. "And you're a rogue FBI agent. Nice to meet you."

"I'm Seth Hammond, and for the sake of full disclosure, I used to be a con man, but I'm no longer involved in that deceptive art." The sharp-featured man grinned at her like a used-car salesman.

Great. Just great.

"And I'm Mark Fitzpatrick," the other man said with a

mild smile that made him look like a choirboy, especially standing next to the former flimflam man with the friendly grin. "I was never a con man, for the record."

His dry delivery of the last statement almost made her smile. "I understand you're waiting for me to outline what we have in mind. But before I do so, I need to know something. If you don't like my plan, what do you intend to do about it?"

The Gates agents and the two women exchanged looks for a second. It was Cain Dennison who finally spoke, apparently for them all. "We'll tell you it's idiotic and suggest something that would actually work."

His blunt candor went a long way toward calming McKenna's rattled nerves. "Fair enough." She waved at the table, pulling up one of the kitchen chairs. "So, let's get started."

THE PLAN SEEMED to pass muster with the other agents, Darcy saw with some relief. He knew it wasn't a foolproof plan, but what plans ever were? McKenna's explanation of how she planned to tap into local video feeds to give them the equivalent of an early-warning system raised the eyebrows of both Sara Lindsey and Ivy Calhoun, the two cops in the room. But neither woman commented.

"We're trying to figure out which man brings backup and which one tries to meet me alone."

"Don't you think they'll suspect a setup?" Sara Lindsey asked.

"They may," McKenna conceded. "But if either of them is connected to the Blue Ridge Infantry, he'll try to lure me out of hiding rather than bring in the FBI. Because they don't know how much I know about what the BRI is up to. That's why I was targeted for death in the first place."

Her answer was met with tense silence at first. Then Sutton Calhoun stood to face them. "Make the calls."

McKenna turned to look at Darcy. "We've selected two rendezvous points," she told the others. "One is the Econo-Tel Motor Lodge just south of Poe Creek. Do you know it?"

Sara Lindsey nodded. "I worked a case near there recently."

"Then you can cover us there. Darcy's going to be with you," McKenna said.

Darcy stared at her. "You want us to split up?"

She caught his arm and took him aside, ignoring the curious looks from the others as they left the kitchen and entered the nearby hallway. "Look, I'm operating on a very thin layer of trust, as it is. We have two bases to cover, and I need someone I trust covering one of them while I take the other. I don't trust any of them. But I trust you."

He didn't know whether to kiss her or shake her. "But you trust them to cover your back?"

"I can cover my own back if need be. What I can't do is cover both feeds. I need you to make sure nobody screws this up. We have to know which man is the turncoat in the FBI. I need your eyes on the feed at the Econo-Tel."

He wanted to argue, but he knew she was right. For the plan to work, they had to have an advance look at both men and who, if anyone, they brought with them for backup.

"Okay. But I don't want you taking any chances. Understood?"

She nodded, and they returned to the kitchen.

"Everything settled?" Mark Fitzpatrick asked.

"Yes," McKenna answered. "As I was saying, Darcy will join Deputy Lindsey and Dennison at the Econo-Tel. One more of you will need to go with them."

"I'll go," Mark Fitzpatrick offered.

Darcy frowned.

"Or not," Fitz muttered.

"I think our friend Darcy is uncertain if I can truly be trusted," Hammond drawled, shooting Darcy an unoffended smile. At least, Darcy thought he looked unoffended. Seth Hammond had been a confidence man for years; even now, it was hard to know exactly what the man was thinking. "I'll go with him. The Boy Scout here can go with the lady."

Fitz rolled his eyes at Seth but gave a nod. "Calhoun, Ivy and I'll go with Mac."

"Our second rendezvous point is the Blackberry Café in Brightwater."

"I know where that is," Sutton Calhoun said with a nod.

"I don't want to confront either man," Darcy said, pressing his palm against the small of McKenna's back. "Understood? This is purely a reconnaissance mission. We're trying to figure out who has put Mac in danger. Then we can see about going to the authorities with what we know."

He felt McKenna's muscles tighten beneath his fingertips, but she didn't argue.

Dennison reached into his pocket and pulled out a cell phone. "I thought you might need another burner phone." He held it out to McKenna.

After a brief hesitation, she took it from him. "Thank you."

"There's a pay phone outside the Econo-Tel," Darcy said. "Mac's going to make the phone call to Cade Landry from there, then ride with Fitz to the café in Brightwater. Seth, you can ride shotgun with me."

As they split up to head for their cars, Darcy caught Sutton's arm on the way out, keeping an eye on McKenna as she followed Mark Fitzpatrick to his truck. "Whose cabin is this?"

"Belongs to Seth's mother. She's over in Nashville for the week visiting her cousin. Seth figured nobody from the FBI would think to connect this place to you."

Darcy nodded, hoping he was right.

Seth was waiting by the passenger door of the Land

Rover, smiling at Darcy across the top of the cab. "You don't trust me a bit, do you?"

"I barely trust anyone at the moment," Darcy answered.

"But especially not me."

Darcy didn't speak.

Seth shrugged. "I get it. I get it all the time, actually. But I reckon you'll just have to see for yourself whether or not I'm worthy of your trust."

"It would behoove you to be so."

Seth smiled as Darcy used the remote to unlock the doors. "Nice accent. You should hear my Irish one." He climbed into the passenger seat.

Darcy looked across the yard toward Fitz's truck. McKenna was standing next to the door, gazing at him across the dark yard. There was just enough moonlight to make out the glitter of her eyes.

Darcy smiled. He saw the slight curve of her lips, the faint glint of her teeth. Then she got into the truck, disappearing from his view.

For a moment, his stomach gave a sickening downward lurch.

He took a deep breath, gathering his wits. He hadn't seen her for eight years. They'd both survived the separation.

They would both survive a couple of hours apart, right?

At least, he hoped so.

CADE LANDRY ANSWERED on the second ring, his voice raspy and thick. "Yeah?"

Great, McKenna thought. Had he been drinking? "Landry, it's Rigsby."

There was a long pause on the other end of the line. For a second, she thought the call had been cut off and started digging in her pocket for quarters to feed the pay phone. Then Landry spoke again. "Where are you?"

"I need to meet you. I don't feel safe."

"Are you hurt?"

"Not badly," she answered, glancing over her shoulder at the Land Rover parked behind her. She couldn't see Darcy's face behind the glare from the motel sign bouncing off the windshield. But she felt his gaze on her. It warmed her, made her feel strong and weak at the same time.

"Tell me where to find you." Landry's voice was stronger now. Didn't sound nearly as slurred. "Are you alone?"

"I am," she lied. "Do you know where the Econo-Tel Motor Lodge is on Route 4 south of Poe Creek?"

"No, but I'll find it. Are you out of sight?"

"Not right now, but I will be as soon as I get off the phone."

"Good. Stay out of sight. You're in serious danger."

"I know. That's why I'm calling you. I need help coming in."

"I'll give it to you. You just get hidden and stay put. I'm in a black Malibu—remember what my car looks like?"

"I remember."

"I'll pull in the parking lot at the motel. Is there someplace you can hide where you can still see the parking lot?"

"Yes," she answered.

"Good. I'm on my way. Get out of sight and I'll see you soon."

She hung up the pay phone and walked over to the Land Rover. Darcy lowered the window and looked up at her. "Landry's coming?"

"Yes." She looked past him at Seth Hammond, whose used-car-salesman grin had disappeared now that the assignment was under way. "How's the video feed holding up?"

He met her gaze steadily. "Clear as a bell. This feed covers the parking lot perfectly. We should be able to spot the target as soon as he shows up."

"What's he driving?" Darcy asked.

"Black Malibu. Later model. It's not a bucar," she added, referring to an FBI fleet vehicle. "It's his personal car."

"Wouldn't he drive an FBI fleet car if he was playing this by the book?" Darcy asked.

"I don't know," she admitted. "Landry's an odd bird. And he loves that car. Just—keep an eye out for any sort of tricks."

"That's what we're here for," Seth said with a slight smile. He looked like an ordinary guy, she thought, when he wasn't trying so hard to play the role of the smarmy con man.

"I've got to hurry to the diner to make the second call," she said, patting the window frame as she started to turn to go.

Darcy caught her hand, holding her in place. "Be careful." His thumb slid over the back of her hand in a caress. "Don't take chances."

She turned her hand over until her palm pressed against his. "Everything in life's a chance. But I'll be careful."

"You do that." He let go of her hand, and she turned away, walking slowly back to join Mark Fitzpatrick in his truck.

Fitz, as he'd told her to call him, started the truck as she buckled herself in. "You ready for this?"

She nodded. "I appreciate this. That you're putting yourself on the line for me when you don't even know me."

"I know Darcy. He and the guys at The Gates helped me out not long ago when someone I know was in trouble. Darcy went to bat for her with Quinn. She needed a job and Darcy made sure Quinn gave her a chance. I don't think even Darcy knows how much he helped her."

"Your girl?" she asked, reading between the lines.

Fitz's lips curved, the boyish smile carving dimples in his cheeks. "Yeah. We're getting married soon." His smile faded. "So, let's get this done right tonight, okay? No surprises. No risks. I kind of promised her I'd come home alive. If I don't, she'll kill me."

"I'm all for coming home alive," she assured him, remembering Darcy's long, deep gaze at her as she walked away from the Land Rover.

They reached the Blackberry Café within ten minutes, parking near the edge of the lot where the glow from the street lamp on the corner didn't quite reach. The pay phone bolted to the wall of the hardware store was barely visible under the shadow of the store awning. It had been in working order when she and Darcy had checked it the night before, but a lot could have changed in a day.

She fed coins into the slot and sent up a silent prayer as she called SSA Darryl Boyle's cell-phone number.

It rang three times without Boyle answering. As she was about to hang up and start over, he picked up. "Boyle."

"Agent Boyle, it's Agent Rigsby. I'm in trouble and I need your help."

Chapter Seventeen

"They don't really think you're clueless about what they're up to, do they?" Olivia lowered the binoculars and turned to look at Quinn.

He shrugged. "I don't think they're actively trying to deceive me, no."

"The woman doesn't want you in on it."

"She doesn't trust me. Or anyone, I assume. She believes her own people were involved in trying to kill her." Quinn took the binoculars Olivia had set down and lifted them to his eyes. Through the lenses, he made out Darcy's Land Rover sitting at one end of the motel's parking lot. "What are they doing?"

"Hammond seems to be on a laptop computer," Olivia answered, drumming her fingers on the dashboard as if impatient for him to hand over the binoculars again.

Quinn ignored her jitters, trying to see if he could discern what was on the computer screen by focusing on the reflection in the Land Rover's passenger-side window. "They seem to be monitoring some kind of video feed."

"Did they set up hidden cameras somewhere?"

"I'm not sure. But I know how to find out." He handed her the binoculars and picked up his cell phone, dialing a number.

Seth Hammond answered on the second ring. "Yeah, boss?"

"Why are you parked in the Econo-Tel Motor Lodge parking lot, monitoring a video feed?"

Hammond muttered a profanity.

A moment later, Nick Darcy's voice was in Quinn's ear. "This isn't your business. Stay out of it."

"She didn't want you to come to me for help?"

"No."

"I'll keep my distance. But are you sure you're prepared for any contingency?"

Darcy's voice tightened, betraying his doubts. "There's no such thing as being prepared for any contingency."

"What are you hoping will happen?"

"We need to know who she can or can't trust at the FBI."

"And how is sitting in a vehicle looking at a video feed going to clarify that question for you?"

"You don't know what our plan involves, Quinn. And I'm not going to tell you." Darcy hung up the phone.

"You have such a way with your employees," Olivia murmured as he pocketed his phone.

"They've set up some sort of trap," Quinn said, reaching for the binoculars. "But Agent Rigsby is nowhere in sight."

"I spotted Dennison and his deputy girlfriend parked on the other side of the motel lot," Olivia commented. "Do we know who else is involved in this mysterious sting?"

"No. Ever since word got around of the GPS trackers in the agents' cars, they've been disabling them."

"Good for them," Olivia murmured, slanting a dark look his way. "We were wrong to try to track them like pets with microchips."

"Knowing where my agents are at the moment might come in very handy." Quinn considered what he knew about the agents he had in sight. Seth Hammond was with

Darcy. And Dennison had brought his girlfriend along for the operation, which meant they weren't necessarily sticking to agents from The Gates alone.

"Sutton Calhoun and his wife," he said aloud a moment later. "Calhoun and Hammond are close now. Rigsby must be with them."

"Just the three of them?"

"Probably one more agent to match the number here. There must be a second stakeout point."

"But where?"

Quinn picked up his phone and dialed Calhoun's cell-phone number. It rang three times before going to voice mail.

"Darcy warned them. They're screening calls from me."

"So what now?" Olivia asked.

Quinn picked up the binoculars and raised them to his eyes again. "They're staking out this parking lot for a reason. Right?"

"Right. You said you think they've set up some sort of trap. But who are they trying to trap?"

Quinn scanned the parking lot. "Rigsby claims there's someone inside the FBI gunning for her. Maybe they settled on a suspect."

"Or two," Olivia pointed out. "Since there's a second stakeout point?"

"One of them is Landry," Quinn said, slanting a look at Olivia.

"I know."

"Any thoughts on the other one?"

Her eyes narrowed as she peered through the windshield. "Darcy asked me some questions about what happened in Richmond. Specifically, he wanted to know who the incident commander for my SWAT unit was."

"Who was it?"

"Darryl Boyle."

"Rigsby's direct supervisor at the Knoxville office?"

"That's the one."

STAKEOUTS WERE GENERALLY boring affairs. Until they weren't.

Except for the call from Quinn twenty minutes earlier, Darcy's stakeout of the Econo-Tel Motor Lodge had been uneventful. If Landry was on his way to meet McKenna, he was taking his own sweet time.

Meanwhile, Darcy felt as if he was about to crawl right out of his skin. His nerves were jittering, his pulse pounding a heightened cadence in his ears, and every twitch of a leaf rustled by the night breeze outside set him on high alert.

He shouldn't have let McKenna convince him to split up. He should be with her instead of staying here watching a silent parking lot.

"Is that a phone?" Seth Hammond's drawl broke the silence in the Land Rover.

Darcy jerked at the noise. "What?"

"I'm hearing a phone ringing."

Darcy listened. Seth was right. A phone was ringing.

"The pay phone," Seth said.

It rang one more time, then went silent.

Darcy looked at Seth. "Coincidence?"

The other man shook his head. "Not damn likely."

The phone started to ring again.

As Darcy started to open the driver's door, Seth put a hand on his arm.

"What if someone's trying to draw you out in the open?"

"What if it's Landry trying to contact her again?" Darcy asked.

"You answering the phone isn't exactly going to make him feel real good about showing up for this shindig."

"It's a chance I have to take." Darcy opened the door

and hurried toward the ringing phone, catching it on the fifth trill. "Hello?"

There was silence on the other end of the line, but Darcy could feel someone listening.

"Hello?" he repeated.

"You're Nick Darcy, right?" The voice on the other end of the line was a deep drawl, broader and gentler than the hard-edged mountain twangs Darcy had grown used to hearing in this part of Tennessee. "This was a setup, wasn't it?"

Darcy didn't answer.

"Doesn't matter," Landry continued, sounding frustrated. "I need to talk to Rigsby. Now."

Cold crept up Darcy's spine and settled in his chest. "I can pass a message along to her."

Landry muttered a low curse. "She's not there, is she?"

"If you'll tell me your message—"

"He knows, Darcy. Darryl Boyle knows it's a setup. And wherever Rigsby's luring him, he's not going there alone."

The chill spread to Darcy's limbs. He clutched the phone more tightly. "You mean he's bringing FBI backup. Right?"

"I don't think so," Landry warned, his voice tight with tension. "Something's not right with him."

"Something's not right with you, either. I've talked to Ava Trent. I've even talked to your old SWAT team partner, Olivia Sharp."

"You talked to Olivia?" There was a shift in the tone of Landry's voice that caught Darcy by surprise.

"They both seem to think you're a dead-ender. On your way back down the ladder before you flame out for good."

Landry was silent for so long, Darcy feared he'd hung up. When he finally spoke again, his voice was flat and weary. "I guess I deserve that. But I'm tellin' you right now, you gotta get Rigsby out of there. I called Boyle. Told him about my call from Rigsby. He said he got one, too, and I should sit tight. He'd take care of it. But something about the way he was talking— I don't know. It didn't sound right. So I called the Knoxville Field Office, offered the Johnson City RA's assistance in the extraction. And nobody in Knoxville knew what the hell I was talking about."

"How do I know you're not setting us both up?" Darcy asked, trying to keep his head as his heart clamored at him to go get McKenna and take her somewhere so far away nobody could find her again.

"You don't," Landry said. Then the line went dead.

Darcy hung up the phone and ran back to the car. "Get Calhoun on the phone," he ordered, already dialing the number of the burner phone he'd given McKenna. The cell phone rang once and went straight to voice mail. "Damn it!"

"Calhoun's not answering," Seth said, looking at Darcy with a worried expression. "What the hell is happening?"

"I'm not sure," Darcy admitted, dialing another number. "But we need to pull up stakes and get to Brightwater as fast as we can."

On the second ring, Alexander Quinn answered. "Ready to talk to me now?"

"Yes," Darcy snapped. "So listen very carefully, because we may already be out of time."

MCKENNA LOOKED AT her watch. Only four minutes had passed since the last time she'd checked. It felt more like an hour. "Maybe we should check in with Calhoun and his wife," she suggested, glancing at Fitz in the driver's seat. "See if they've seen anything suspicious."

"I'm sure they'd have called us if they had," Fitz said reasonably.

"I'm climbing out of my skin here. Can't we just call someone? Anyone? Maybe we could call Darcy and see if his crew has seen anything from Landry."

Fitz looked her way, amusement crinkling the corners of his eyes. "You try Darcy. I'll call Calhoun."

She tugged the burner phone from her jacket pocket and dialed the number he'd stored for her.

Nothing happened. She looked at the display and saw there were no bars. The phone wasn't receiving any signal from the cell tower.

"Hmm," Fitz murmured.

"What?"

"No reception."

Alarms blared in her head. "We were able to check in with Calhoun just fifteen minutes ago. The signal was great."

"I know." Fitz frowned.

McKenna looked down at her laptop, checking the video feed. There was nothing new there. She could see Calhoun's truck parked at the other end of the small shopping strip in one of the diner's security cameras. Fitz's truck was still visible in the feed from the second camera. Nothing had changed.

She narrowed her eyes and reached for the power-window switch on the passenger door.

"What are you doing?"

She reached out the passenger window and waved toward the camera, keeping her eye on the feed.

Nothing in the image on her computer screen changed. No hand, no wave.

"Oh, hell." She raised the window again and pulled her Glock from the holster behind her back.

"What?"

"Someone's hacked our feed. They're out there." She peered out the window at the quiet street in front of the diner, looking for any sign of movement. "And I don't think it's the FBI."

Fitz muttered a curse and started the truck's engine. As he

put the vehicle in Reverse, a hard thud shook the chassis, and the truck began to shimmy as Fitz tried to steer it backward.

"Son of a bitch," he growled. "Someone shot out a tire."

"Drive anyway!" McKenna twisted in her seat, trying to see behind them. The road appeared deserted, but out of the corner of her eye, she saw a rush of movement toward her.

The truck came to a hard stop, flinging her against the seat belt and sending the baseball cap covering her curls flying onto the dashboard. Her hair tumbled into her face, blinding her for crucial seconds.

When she shoved her hair out of her eyes again, she was staring down the barrel of a shotgun. Her heart sank as she recognized the shaggy-haired man with cold blue eyes gazing back at her from behind the weapon.

Calvin Hopkins. Current head of the eastern Tennessee branch of the Blue Ridge Infantry. As cold and nasty a son of a bitch as she'd come across in a long, long time.

The man she'd hoped to bring down by going undercover.

"Hey there, Maggie." He bared his teeth at her in a parody of a smile. "Or should I call you McKenna?"

THE DINER WAS DESERTED. No sign of Fitz, Calhoun or the women. No sign, in fact, that anyone had been here recently at all. Until the headlights of Darcy's Land Rover swept over a shard of tire tread near the far end of the shopping-strip parking lot.

He put the Land Rover in Park and got out, bending to examine the tread. It had been pitted by buckshot, he realized. Several bits of shot remained in the rubber tread.

Fear rose like bile in his throat. He swallowed with difficulty, trying to maintain control over his emotions. Panic wouldn't help anyone.

Panic got people killed.

"Is that buckshot?" Seth Hammond's tone was uncharacteristically serious. "Son of a—"

Darcy pulled out his cell phone and dialed Sutton Calhoun's number. He heard a trilling sound coming from somewhere nearby.

Seth crossed to the front of the diner and crouched by one of the bushes that flanked the walkway into the diner. He rose again, now holding the ringing phone, his expression grim. "Sutton's."

"Damn it." Darcy raked his hand through his hair, furious and terrified at the same time. He should have made her reconsider her crazy plan. He should have insisted on being with her.

"Don't waste time second-guessing yourself, man." Seth put his hand briefly on Darcy's shoulder. "We've got to figure out where they've taken them and get them back."

If they're even still alive, Darcy thought, his heart pounding with dread.

Chapter Eighteen

McKenna had no idea where the others were. Whether they were even alive. Frankly, she was surprised Calvin Hopkins hadn't blown her away on sight. But apparently he wasn't the one calling the shots.

Darryl Boyle was.

"Whom have you involved besides Darcy?" Boyle leaned against the wall of the cellar where she was being held, his arms folded and his expression placid. He spoke in a slow, measured tone, his Baltimore accent mostly neutralized, coming out only now and then in his vowels. They could have been sitting across from each other at the Knoxville Field Office, calmly discussing the latest case.

Except she was tied to a water pipe, her feet duct-taped together and two loaded shotguns aimed at her, wielded by bushy-bearded, cold-eyed Blue Ridge Infantry members flanking Boyle.

Jutting her chin toward him, she forced herself to smile. "Do your boys here know what you're really up to?"

"My boys, as you call them, are sovereign citizens and answer only to themselves. Don't you, boys?"

They both nodded.

"He's using you," McKenna said. "He's goading you into doing what he wants, and then he's going to make an example of you. Crack down on sovereign citizens like

yourselves because he thinks you pose a dangerous threat
to the government you hate so much. The government he
works for."

"The boys know you're the government plant, Rigsby."
Boyle's smile was placid. Almost friendly.

He was so sure of himself, she realized. So certain he
had everything under control.

Except he didn't. If he really had everything under control, she'd already be dead. There was something he wanted
from her, and she had a sick feeling it had everything to
do with Nick Darcy.

"Who else is involved besides Darcy?" Boyle repeated.
"The Gates, I presume. Considering who you were with
when we found you."

"What did you do to them?" she asked, her heart in her
throat. If Fitz, Calhoun and Ivy were dead because of her—

"They're enjoying the hospitality of our friends in the
BRI," he said with a feral smile that made her skin crawl.

"You can't kill us all," she growled. "Too many people
know what's really going on."

"Just a few, really. Your friend Darcy and the people he
has with him at the Econo-Tel Motor Lodge."

Terror poured through her body like ice water. He knew
where Darcy was staked out?

Was Darcy even still alive?

Boyle walked closer, bending to look her in the eye. He
had warm brown eyes, the same color as Darcy's. But behind the manufactured friendliness lurked a cold hatred
she'd never noticed before. He spoke in a soft, even kind
tone, but it sent a shudder up her spine. "I need you to tell
me if you've contacted anyone else."

"I'm not telling you anything."

"Yes. You will." He motioned over the man on the right.
The bearded man came over quickly, the shotgun still point-

ing at her chest. "Keller, show our guest what buckshot can do to a knee—"

A banging sound on the door to the cellar caught the attention of all three men. McKenna felt her whole body go hot, cold, then hot again with sheer relief as the man named Keller swung the barrel of his shotgun away from her.

"Trouble's comin'," the voice on the other side of the door called. "All hands needed."

Boyle nodded toward the two men. "Go. I'll watch her."

They climbed the stairs and disappeared through the cellar door, leaving McKenna alone with Boyle.

"I guess your friends tracked us down." He grabbed a metal folding chair leaning against the wall, unfolded it and set it in front of her. He sat down, crossing one leg over the other. "Wonder how they did that."

"Darcy knows the BRI is behind what happened to me. And he works for The Gates, who seem to have made taking the BRI down a personal project."

"I have nothing against The Gates or their agents," Boyle said calmly, "but they're a small group with limited influence. They may eventually take down the BRI, but other groups will continue rising up in their place. It's like trying to take down a jumbo jet with a peashooter. Something big needs to catch the attention of the public. Then the public will press Congress—"

"You're willing to sacrifice thousands of people just to change public sentiment about domestic terrorism? You're sanctioning the very thing you're trying to stop!"

"Wars have casualties."

"It's a war you've started!"

"Not true. Look at Oklahoma City. The Olympics bombing."

"Isolated acts. It's not a pattern."

"You don't see the pattern because you've blinded yourself to the reality." He leaned forward, his eyes alight with passion. "It's not just the big bold acts, Rigsby. Do you know how many police officers die at the hands of so-called sovereign citizens like our friends Keller and Shelton out there? Scores every year."

"In a nation of over three hundred million," McKenna protested.

"Whom have you involved besides Darcy, Agent Rigsby?"

She pressed her lips together, not answering.

THERE ARE TEN men in the compound, but if they get on the horn, they can probably bring in thirty or forty more," Alexander Quinn warned Darcy as they surveyed the BRI enclave in the heart of Bridal Veil Woods near the tiny town of Thurlow's Gap. Four families linked to the Blue Ridge Infantry lived in small, well-fortified cabins in the woods nestled between two mountains in the southernmost part of Ridge County. Those cabins were now barely visible in the faint light of dawn rising over the mountains in the east.

"They probably have already," Seth warned, nodding toward sudden movement outside the small compound. Several men armed with shotguns and rifles had gathered in front of the houses like a phalanx of palace guards.

"This kind of situation never ends well for anybody," Seth warned. He was crouched beside Darcy, viewing the scene through a pair of high-powered binoculars. "Waco, Ruby Ridge—"

"There has to be a way to get her out of there," Darcy said gruffly. "We just have to figure it out."

"Boyle isn't their friend." Cain Dennison spoke for the first time since they'd set up in their surveillance position atop Thurlow Rise, east of the conclave. Next to him, his dark-eyed fiancée was checking the magazine of a compact Kel-Tec PF-9.

Darcy wondered what had become of McKenna's Glock. What had become of her...

He made himself focus. She was still alive. He could feel it, like a second heartbeat in his own chest. She was alive and she was looking for a chance to get free.

He had to figure out a way to give her that chance.

"I'm going down there alone," he said aloud.

The other agents in earshot all turned to look at him as if he'd lost his mind.

"No, you're not," Quinn said, his tone dismissive.

"Hear me out. They have Calhoun and his wife. Mark Fitzpatrick. And McKenna. They don't know who else might be helping her. Except me. They know about me because Darryl Boyle knows about me. The FBI has been looking into her connection with me. I can go down there. We can use that buttonhole camera you brought—"

"They might shoot on sight."

"They want to know what we know. Boyle needs to have plausible deniability with the FBI. Right now, it's our word against his. Nobody's seen him with any BRI members. It's all speculation. But he knows we brought in some of the Gates agents."

"What if Rigsby's already spilled everything she knows?" Sara Lindsey asked.

Darcy shot her a pointed look. "She'd die before she'd give up anything."

"I hope she doesn't have to," Sara responded, a grim look on her pretty face. But the look in her eyes was more sympathetic than Darcy had expected.

"Do it."

The quiet response from Alexander Quinn drew their attention his way. He was looking toward the enclave below, his eyes narrowed. A moment later, he turned and pinned Darcy with his sharp gaze. "You know the stakes. You're invested. Do it."

"Any idea how we're supposed to get him in there without them shooting him on sight?" Sara asked.

"Wave the white flag?" Seth suggested.

Darcy grimaced. "Surrender?"

"Those men down there are a bunch of thickheaded cowards, but they think of themselves as honorable, patriotic men," Seth said with quiet urgency. "They'll hesitate to shoot an unarmed man turning himself in to them."

"Hesitate," Sara reiterated. "But that doesn't mean they won't shoot, sooner or later."

"It's a risk I'm willing to take," Darcy said, unclipping the holster from his jeans. He handed the pistol and holster to Quinn. "Can we contact them? Get me in there?"

"I know at least one of them. Randall Farmer. I ran some cons with him over in Barrowville," Seth said. "I can contact him, see if I can get through to Calvin Hopkins. He's taken the reins of this cell since Billy Dawson went to jail for that mass-poisoning attempt."

"Make it happen," Darcy said.

DARRYL BOYLE GOT up from the metal folding chair and started pacing slowly in front of McKenna, a faint smile on his face. "I suppose we must assume your friends have found Calvin and his boys."

"And you," she said.

"They think I'm one of them." He smiled more broadly. "That's what undercover is really about, Rigsby. Selling yourself as one of them. You never could pull off that part."

Because I'm not a raving lunatic like you, she thought, her stomach twisting. She'd worked with Darryl Boyle for over a year. Took his advice, spent long hours in research and discussions with him, even socialized with him now and then with other field-office agents and personnel.

She hadn't had a clue that he'd lost his bloody mind.

She had to get out of here. As soon as possible.

Another knock on the cellar door set her nerves rattling again.

"What do you want?" Boyle snapped.

It was Calvin Hopkins himself who walked through the cellar door and down the rough-hewn wooden steps. He slanted a hard look at McKenna before turning to Boyle. "Darcy wants to talk."

DARCY FELT EYES on him before he made it ten feet onto Calvin Hopkins's property, but he tried not to let his twitching nerves show. He had one chance to get this right. One chance to stay alive and get McKenna safely out of here.

He just had to get on the inside somehow. Get to her and make sure she was still alive, then work the angle he and Quinn had discussed while Seth was on the phone with Randall Farmer.

Dew clung to the legs of his jeans as he climbed the grassy hill. A hundred yards up the rise, the line of armed militia members came into view. And though Darcy had known they were there, had prepared himself for the sight of them, his blood still froze when he saw a dozen gun barrels pointed straight at his heart.

"Hands up," ordered one of the men.

Darcy stopped and raised his hands. "I'm unarmed."

The man who'd spoken nodded toward Darcy. "Check him out."

Another man, younger and clean-shaven, handed his rifle to the man next to him and crossed to Darcy. He patted him down, his touch less rough than Darcy had expected. Darcy gave him a considering look as the man backed away, his curiosity piqued. But he didn't have time to figure out why. The older man, the one clearly in charge, motioned him forward.

He walked slowly toward the gun line, half expecting with each step to walk right into a volley of rifle fire. But the BRI members held their fire.

"I'm Cal," the older man said, flashing a disarming smile. "You're Nick, right?"

"Darcy," he said.

One dark bushy eyebrow rose, but Cal just nodded. "Darcy. I understand you want to talk?"

"I know something you need to know about Darryl Boyle."

"Boyle?" Cal tried to sound puzzled, but he didn't pull it off. "Don't know any Boyle."

"Yes, you do. You think he's your secret weapon. But he's not. He's not your friend. And he's not on your side."

WHAT THE HELL was Darcy thinking, coming here? And alone, if the snippets of overheard conversation between Boyle and Calvin Hopkins could be believed.

Boyle came back down the stairs slowly, a smile on his face. But McKenna was beginning to read the SSA a little better, now that she had the key to understanding him.

He was obsessive and narcissistic. But he was also in a very vulnerable position where the BRI was concerned. And like any vulnerable man faced with an unexpected wrinkle in his plan, he was showing signs of stress. Sweat beading on his brow. A nervous twitch to his gaze, as if he was afraid to let it settle too long on any given point.

"What are they going to do to Darcy?" she asked.

"Talk. For now."

And that was what Boyle was afraid of, she realized. That Darcy would say the wrong thing, reveal the wrong fact about Boyle's real reason for rubbing elbows with the Blue Ridge Infantry.

"He doesn't know about you," she lied.

"You didn't tell him?" Boyle looked skeptical.

"I told him about Landry. I didn't mention you. I was hoping I was wrong about you, and nobody else would have to know. I respected you. Your record, your work."

His eyes narrowed. "I don't believe you."

She shrugged. "I can't do anything to change your mind."

"You can tell me how many other people are out there right now."

"I have no clue. Darcy was my only contact until last night. He's the one who brought the others into this mess. I didn't want anyone else involved."

Her words had the ring of truth, and she could tell Boyle knew it. "So they think Landry's the one behind all of this."

"They did. And if you stay out of sight, they'll continue to think so. But if anything happens to Darcy, his friends won't stop looking for answers." She tried not to let her fear show. "You need to tell Calvin to send Darcy packing back where he came from."

"That's touching, really. Trying to protect your friend." Boyle's eyes glinted with curiosity. "Or maybe he's more than a friend?"

So much more, she thought with despair, and she hadn't ever had the guts to say it out loud. "Make him think I've been taken somewhere else. He'll go looking for me, and then you'll be rid of him."

"You'd give up your own life to save him?"

She shook her head, suddenly terrified by the gleam of understanding in the SSA's eyes. "I didn't say that. I'm trying to get out of here alive, too, believe me. Darcy's got a lot of people who'll look for him. I don't. Thanks to you, everybody thinks I'm a crooked fed. Nobody's going to care what happens to me. So I can help you with your plans. And then, I hope, you'll let me go free. What am I going to do, tell the FBI I helped you commit an act of terror? They already think I've gone native with the BRI, right?"

He nodded slowly.

"Get Darcy out of here, and then I'll help you with whatever you're up to. Just give me my life in return, and I'll disappear. Nobody will ever see me again."

"I don't believe you," he said again. But this time, she heard a hint of uncertainty.

"Fine. Let Darcy get taken prisoner or worse. Then you'll wish you'd never heard his name. Because there are people out there, very powerful people, who haven't forgotten he's the son of an influential former US ambassador. He has friends in very high places. And they won't stop trying to find out what happened to him until they have all the answers."

Boyle held her gaze for a moment before he looked away. Slowly, he crossed the small room and started climbing the steps.

But before he got there, the door opened and Calvin Hopkins filled the doorway. "Just the man I was looking for," he said, a feral grin splitting his bearded face.

Boyle took a step back, almost losing his balance. But Hopkins grabbed him by the front of his shirt, jerked him through the door and shut it behind them with a loud slam.

The ensuing silence seemed thick and oppressive. Left alone for the first time since they'd brought her to the cellar, McKenna started twisting the rope holding her tied to the water pipe, trying to loosen the knots enough to give her a chance of breaking free.

For several minutes, the only thing she heard was her own accelerated breathing and the rasp of the hemp rope against the metal pipes as she struggled to loosen her restraints. But as she felt the bindings finally begin to loosen around her raw wrists, she heard a furtive *snick* sound, followed by the quiet thud of footsteps on the wooden stairs.

She looked up, blinking away the sweat dripping into her eyes. Blinked again to be sure she was really seeing what she thought she was.

"Darcy?"

He came the rest of the way down the steps quickly, hurrying to her side. "Are you all right?"

"How did you get in here?"

"I did someone named Cal a favor. Calvin Hopkins, I presume." He tugged at the knots around her wrists until they finally loosened enough to pull her hands free. He then ripped the duct tape away from her ankles and pulled her to her feet. "We have five minutes to get out of here before they come back from dealing with him. Don't ask questions. Don't look back."

He took her hand and pulled her with him up the steps, pausing only when her knees started to wobble as she reached the top landing. He bent to look at her. "Do you trust me?"

She stared back at him, her heart pounding. "Yes."

He kissed her forehead, his lips lingering for a breathless moment. Then he tugged her hand again. "Let's get you out of here."

Epilogue

Night had fallen over Knoxville, Tennessee, after a long day of debriefing. SAC Robertson had brought in a doctor to check on her gunshot wounds, but she'd talked them both out of admitting her for treatment. "They're practically healed by now," she'd protested, and they'd been able to tell by her stern tone that she wasn't going to agree to any attempts to trundle her off to the hospital for further tests. Besides, the doctor had been forced to concede that Darcy had done a good job of keeping the wounds clean and treated.

"You should follow up with your own doctor in a day or two," the bureau doctor had told her with a firm look before he gathered his supplies and left her alone with Glen Robertson.

The next few hours had been a series of in-depth interviews, not just with Robertson but video interviews with high-ranking officials at FBI headquarters in Washington. She'd told them everything she knew about Darryl Boyle's involvement with the Blue Ridge Infantry, including the fact that she'd been forced to leave him behind when making her escape.

"I suppose that doesn't exactly cover me with glory," she said.

"I'm not sure any of us is in a position to judge your

choices, under the circumstances," Robertson murmured. "And you have no idea where they could have taken Boyle?"

She shook her head. "I don't. There are places in the hills where secrets have stayed hidden for centuries."

Finally, close to 10:00 p.m., apparently everyone interested in what she had to say ran out of questions. The video links shut down and Robertson finally turned to her in the silence of his office.

"I don't think you have a chance in hell of going anywhere in the FBI, Agent Rigsby."

She nodded, unsurprised. "I know."

"It's a damned shame. You're a good agent."

"I'm not. I can't play by the rules enough to be a good FBI agent."

Robertson put his hand lightly on her shoulder. "Maybe not. But I think you did more to stop a terror attack these past few days than you realize."

She hoped so. She just wasn't sure the Blue Ridge Infantry would let one little setback stop them.

"Am I free to go?" she asked.

"You need to stay in the area until the case is officially closed. But yes, you're free to go. Do you need a ride?"

She wasn't sure what had happened to her car. She'd have to see if it was still where she'd left it before everything went crazy, or if it had been towed already. "Yeah, I guess I do."

A little while later, SAC Robertson pulled up in front of her apartment building and let her off at the curb. "You want me to park and walk in with you?"

She couldn't help but laugh. "I think I can probably handle it." She headed up the sidewalk to the awning-covered double doors.

Inside, the apartment lobby was quiet and mostly empty, except for a man sitting on one of the white lobby chairs.

He looked up as she entered, and for a moment, she thought she was seeing what she wanted.

Then he stood, tall and lean and so familiar, her heart started to ache.

"Thought you'd never get here," Darcy said with a smile.

SHE LOOKED TIRED, he thought. No doubt the FBI had put her through the wringer before letting her leave. He'd undergone similar questioning from the Ridge County Sheriff's Department, especially since one of their deputies had been tangentially involved in what had happened the night before.

"I heard you found Fitz, Calhoun and his wife safe and alive."

"They managed to free themselves from the shed where they'd been stashed," Darcy told her, waving off her offer of something to drink. She looked strangely out of place in this clean, utilitarian apartment she apparently called home. Wild-haired, makeup-free and still wearing the grimy clothes she'd been wearing when she was abducted by Hopkins and his crew, she seemed like an alien presence in this city flat.

"Everybody's okay?"

He nodded. "And Quinn took me off paid administrative leave. I've been cleared to resume duties."

She smiled. "Good. About damn time."

"That's what I told him." He fell silent, wondering how to approach the next topic.

Them.

Before he could speak, McKenna grimaced. "I need a shower."

"I could use one, too." He crossed to where she stood by the kitchen counter and took a deep breath before speaking. "We could share."

She looked up at him, smiling as if she thought he was kidding.

He wasn't.

Her smile faded. "You're serious, aren't you?"

"I thought I'd lost you." He touched her face, let his fingers tangle in her hair. "I thought you were dead. And I realized that I've been in love with you for over eight years."

Tears filled her eyes. She let them fall. "Oh, Darcy. I love you, too. I always have. I just didn't think—" She knuckled the tears away.

He tugged her closer. "Didn't think you could put up with such a priggish rule-keeper?"

She laughed. "You are anything but priggish. And I'm pretty sure you broke more rules than I did over the past few days."

"I try."

She touched his face. "I thought you'd never be happy with someone with one foot still in the hills. I am what I am. These hills made me who I am, and I don't know how to be anything else."

"I wouldn't want you to be anything or anyone but exactly who you are." He cradled her face between his hands. "I depend on you being you. I need you, just the way you are. So, tell me. If I said I wanted you to come to Purgatory and be with me for good—could you do it? Would you?"

She tugged him to her, kissing him deeply. He pulled her closer, his heart starting to race as she pushed him back against the kitchen counter.

He dragged his mouth free. "I'll take that as a yes."

She laughed again, the sound beautifully free and light. "That's definitely a yes. And while we're at it—think you can talk Quinn into giving me a job?"

"What about the FBI?"

She arched her eyebrows. "I'd be a dead-ender like Landry."

"Oh," he said. "Did you hear about Landry?"

She shook her head. "SAC Robertson didn't mention him. Did something happen to him?"

"Nobody knows. He didn't show up for work this morning, and when his supervisor sent an agent to check on him, his apartment had been cleared of any personal items. His landlord said he'd paid up the remainder of his lease, told the manager to dispose of the furniture as he saw fit and left."

"Wow. I thought you said he tried to help us."

"I think he did," Darcy admitted. "He seemed honestly worried about you and what Darryl Boyle was up to."

"Robertson said there's no sign of Boyle." Her expression darkened. "I don't know that I feel very good about leaving him to the tender mercies of the BRI."

"I didn't, either," Darcy admitted. "But it was the only way to get you out of there without a standoff. And a standoff with that many armed, reckless men never ends well."

She pressed her cheek against his shoulder. "I was so afraid for you."

"I was so afraid for you, too." He kissed the top of her head. "But we're both safe now."

"Till the next time we butt heads with the BRI." She kissed his shoulder and looked up at him. "Quinn's not through with them, is he?"

"No."

She shot him an impish smile. "Well, we'll worry about that later, okay? We have a shower to take."

"Yes," he agreed, tugging at the hem of her T-shirt, "we do."

She dodged free, laughing. "Race you, Jeeves!"

"Not a Brit!" he protested as she darted toward the hallway.

She stopped in the doorway and turned, gazing at him

with so much happiness it made his chest ache. "You are. You're *my* Brit."

He closed the distance between them, pulling her tightly into his arms. "I guess that makes you my hillbilly, then."

"It does." She wrapped her arms around his neck and pulled him down for a kiss.

* * * * *

Award-winning author Paula Graves's miniseries
THE GATES *continues next month with*
TWO SOULS HOLLOW.
You'll find it wherever
Harlequin Intrigue books are sold!

COMING NEXT MONTH FROM

HARLEQUIN®

INTRIGUE

Available April 21, 2015

#1563 SHOWDOWN AT SHADOW JUNCTION
Big "D" Dads: The Daltons • by Joanna Wayne
When Jade Dalton escapes a ruthless kidnapper on the trail of a multimillion-dollar necklace, Navy SEAL Booker Knox will do whatever it takes to protect the beautiful event planner. Failure isn't an option.

#1564 TWO SOULS HOLLOW
The Gates • by Paula Graves
Ginny Coltrane might hold the key to proving Anson Daughtry's innocence. But when Ginny is dragged into a drug war, Anson may be her only hope of escaping with her life.

#1565 SCENE OF THE CRIME: KILLER COVE
by Carla Cassidy
Accused of murder, Bo McBride has finally returned to Lost Lagoon to clear his name—with the help of sexy Claire Silver. But as they investigate, it doesn't take long to realize that danger stalks Claire...

#1566 NAVY SEAL JUSTICE
Covert Cowboys, Inc. • by Elle James
After former Navy SEAL James Monahan and FBI agent Melissa Bradley's mutual friend goes missing, they join forces to find him. But as a band of dangerous criminals closes in, survival means trusting each other—their toughest mission yet.

#1567 COWBOY INCOGNITO
The Brothers of Hastings Ridge Ranch • by Alice Sharpe
A roadtrip to uncover Zane Doe's identity exposes his *real* connection to Kinsey Frost—and the murderous intentions of those once close to her. Now Zane must protect her from someone who wants to silence her for good.

#1568 UNDER SUSPICION
Bayou Bonne Chance • by Mallory Kane
Undercover NSA agent Zach Winters vows to solve his best friend's murder. With the criminals closing in, Zach will risk his own life to protect a vulnerable widow and her beautiful bodyguard, Madeleine Tierney—the woman he can't imagine saying goodbye to.

YOU CAN FIND MORE INFORMATION ON UPCOMING HARLEQUIN® TITLES, FREE EXCERPTS AND MORE AT WWW.HARLEQUIN.COM.

HICNM0415

REQUEST YOUR FREE BOOKS!
2 FREE NOVELS PLUS 2 FREE GIFTS!

◆ HARLEQUIN®

INTRIGUE®

BREATHTAKING ROMANTIC SUSPENSE

YES! Please send me 2 FREE Harlequin Intrigue® novels and my 2 FREE gifts (gifts are worth about $10). After receiving them, if I don't wish to receive any more books, I can return the shipping statement marked "cancel." If I don't cancel, I will receive 6 brand-new novels every month and be billed just $4.74 per book in the U.S. or $5.24 per book in Canada. That's a savings of at least 14% off the cover price! It's quite a bargain! Shipping and handling is just 50¢ per book in the U.S. and 75¢ per book in Canada.* I understand that accepting the 2 free books and gifts places me under no obligation to buy anything. I can always return a shipment and cancel at any time. Even if I never buy another book, the two free books and gifts are mine to keep forever.

182/382 HDN F42N

Name	(PLEASE PRINT)

Address	Apt. #

City	State/Prov.	Zip/Postal Code

Signature (if under 18, a parent or guardian must sign)

Mail to the Harlequin® Reader Service:
IN U.S.A.: P.O. Box 1867, Buffalo, NY 14240-1867
IN CANADA: P.O. Box 609, Fort Erie, Ontario L2A 5X3
**Are you a subscriber to Harlequin Intrigue books
and want to receive the larger-print edition?
Call 1-800-873-8635 or visit www.ReaderService.com.**

* Terms and prices subject to change without notice. Prices do not include applicable taxes. Sales tax applicable in N.Y. Canadian residents will be charged applicable taxes. Offer not valid in Quebec. This offer is limited to one order per household. Not valid for current subscribers to Harlequin Intrigue books. All orders subject to credit approval. Credit or debit balances in a customer's account(s) may be offset by any other outstanding balance owed by or to the customer. Please allow 4 to 6 weeks for delivery. Offer available while quantities last.

Your Privacy—The Harlequin® Reader Service is committed to protecting your privacy. Our Privacy Policy is available online at www.ReaderService.com or upon request from the Harlequin Reader Service.

We make a portion of our mailing list available to reputable third parties that offer products we believe may interest you. If you prefer that we not exchange your name with third parties, or if you wish to clarify or modify your communication preferences, please visit us at www.ReaderService.com/consumerschoice or write to us at Harlequin Reader Service Preference Service, P.O. Box 9062, Buffalo, NY 14269. Include your complete name and address.

HI13R

SPECIAL EXCERPT FROM

 HARLEQUIN

I N T R I G U E

Bo McBride, accused but never arrested for the murder of his girlfriend two years ago, has finally returned to Lost Lagoon, Mississippi, to clear his name with Claire Silber's help. But it doesn't take long for them to realize that real danger stalks Claire.

Read on for a sneak preview of
SCENE OF THE CRIME: KILLER COVE,
the latest crime scene book from
New York Times *bestselling author*
Carla Cassidy.

"So, your turn. Tell me what you've been doing for the last two years," Claire asked. "Have you made yourself a new, happy life? Found a new love? I heard through the grapevine that you're living in Jackson now."

Bo nodded at the same time the sound of rain splattered against the window. "I opened a little bar and grill, Bo's Place, although it's nothing like the original." His dark brows tugged together in a frown, as if remembering the highly successful business he'd had here in town before he was ostracized.

He took another big drink and then continued, "There's no new woman in my life. I don't even have friends. Hell, I'm not even sure what I'm doing here with you."

"You're here because I'm a bossy woman," she replied. She got up to refill his glass. "And I thought you could use an extra friend while you're here."

She handed him the fresh drink and then curled back up

in the corner of the sofa. The rain fell steadily now. She turned on the end table lamp as the room darkened with the storm.

For a few minutes they remained silent. She could tell by his distant stare toward the opposite wall that he was lost inside his head.

Despite his somber expression, she couldn't help but feel a physical attraction to him that she'd never felt before. Still, that wasn't what had driven her to seek contact with him, to invite him into her home. She had an ulterior motive.

A low rumble of thunder seemed to pull him out of his head. He focused on her and offered a small smile of apology. "Sorry about that. I got lost in thoughts of everything I need to get done before I leave town."

"I wanted to talk to you about that," she said.

He raised a dark brow. "About all the things I need to take care of?"

"No, about you leaving town."

"What about it?"

She drew a deep breath, knowing she was putting her nose in business that wasn't her own, and yet unable to stop herself. "Doesn't it bother you knowing that Shelly's murderer is still walking these streets, free as a bird?"

His eyes narrowed slightly. "Why are you so sure I'm innocent?" he asked.

Don't miss
SCENE OF THE CRIME: KILLER COVE
by New York Times *bestselling author Carla Cassidy,*
available May 2015 wherever
Harlequin® Intrigue books and ebooks are sold.

www.Harlequin.com

THE WORLD IS BETTER WITH

Romance

Harlequin has everything from contemporary, passionate and heartwarming to suspenseful and inspirational stories.

Whatever your mood,
we have a romance just for you!

Connect with us to find your next great read,
special offers and more.

f /HarlequinBooks

🐦 @HarlequinBooks

www.HarlequinBlog.com

www.Harlequin.com/Newsletters

H HARLEQUIN®

A *Romance* FOR EVERY MOOD™

www.Harlequin.com